THE MUTT MYSTERIES

TO FETCH A VILLAIN

More quirky characters, more twisted plots, and funnier. A good laugh is therapeutic...look it up. These stories are the perfect antidote to our troubled times of viruses, masks, and social distancing. You need to read this book.

~Mike Owens
Author of *Bernie & Bertie*
(Serial Killers Need Love Too)

TO FETCH A SCOUNDREL

"These four tales of intrigue are filled with unexpected twists and delightful dogs who help solve the mysteries and capture the culprits. From the Rottweiler Director of Security, Oliver, to Yorkshires Cagney and Lacey, who prove even tiny terriers can tangle the plans of any evil-doer, you'll love these mysteries."

~Cherie O'Boyle
Author of the *Estela Nogales Mysteries*
and working dog suspense stories

"Dog lovers rejoice! *To Fetch a Scoundrel* is a charming collection of 'tails' by four talented mystery writers."

~Maggie King
Author of the Hazel Rose Book Group Mysteries

TO FETCH A THIEF

"Canines, corpses and clues: A cohesive collection of four compelling mystery novellas where everything—and nothing—is exactly as it seems. A paws-itive delight, and a must-read for dog lovers everywhere."

~Judy Penz Sheluk
Bestselling author of the Glass Dolphin
and Marketville mystery series

———————

"Exceptionally engaging! Each story is funny, smart, page-turning entertainment. A must-read for mystery lovers."

~ Samantha McGraw
Tea Cottage Mysteries

TO FETCH A VILLAIN

Four Fun "Tails" of Miscreants and Murder . . .

Contributing Authors:

Jayne Ormerod

Maria Hudgins

Teresa Inge

Heather Weidner

To Fetch a Villain

Four Fun "Tails" of Miscreants and Murder . . .

Copyright 2020 by
Jayne Ormerod, Maria Hudgins
Teresa Inge, and Heather Weidner

Cover Design by San Coils at CoverKicks.com

ISBN: 9798681709619

Published by
Bay Breeze Publishing
Norfolk, VA

ACKNOWLEDGMENTS

They've done it again. Our furry friends have taken another bite out of crime and gifted us with more laughs and cuddles than we deserve. Again, we have four novellas in a slim volume that will not lose its charm even after it becomes a bit chewed on the corners and, may we add, "dog-eared." Not that any of your pets, dear reader, would ever do such a thing.

For this, the third Mutt Mystery, we have stories with fictional mutts by Teresa Inge (Yorkshire terriers) Maria Hudgins (bichons), Jayne Ormerod (Great Dane), and Heather Weidner (English bulldog). If your own love is not among these, keep reading. Lots of other breeds make it onto these pages in one capacity or another.

We four authors love our pets and understand that they are truly our best friends. More than this, they are smarter than we are. We all know how trained dogs help the police, rescue teams, and shepherds, but regular dogs also have amazing abilities. That little beagle who's not supposed to be on the sofa has a nose that's a hundred thousand times more sensitive than yours. They can sense the presence of certain diseases before the doctor can. They know when we need someone to listen to us. They can sense when a "bad" person is in the room, and they can smell bacon a mile away.

We want to thank San Coils of COVER KICKS for the cover design of this volume. Much appreciation extended to our fellow Sister in Crime, cozy mystery writer Yvonne Saxon, for proofreading our work, and to our first readers for their helpful suggestions.

We are all indebted to the tireless workers in our community animal shelters and to the ASPCA for the good work they do. A portion of the proceeds from the sale of this book are donated to local shelters. And let's not forget our veterinarians who enable our pets to live longer and happier lives than ever before in history.

As always, we thank Sisters in Crime for supporting mystery authors like us. We couldn't do what we do without you.

~Jayne, Maria, Teresa and Heather

TABLE OF CONTENTS

RUFF DAY

By Jayne Ormerod

Darby Agnes Moore owns and operates Ruff Day Doggie Boutique and Dog Wash, a small establishment in the coastal town of Bay Vista, North Carolina. Her top employee is shelter rescue Mr. Belvedere, a one hundred and forty-five-pound Great Dane. Darby takes a huge financial risk when she invests heavily in a local marketing gimmick. Months of planning went into the event. What could possibly go wrong?

It's a *Ruff Day* when Darby and best friend Tianna Platt arrive at the venue and discover a dead body. If that's not trouble enough, Tianna tops the official suspects' list. When Darby and Mr. Belvedere team up to collar the killer, the fur really starts to fly!

JAYNE ORMEROD grew up in a small Ohio town then went on to a small-town Ohio college. Upon earning her degree in accountancy, she became a CIA (that's not a sexy spy thing, but a Certified Internal Auditor.) She married a naval officer and off they sailed to see the world. After nineteen moves, they, along with their two rescue dogs Tiller and Scout, have settled into a cozy cottage by the sea. Jayne's publishing credits include two novels, five novellas, and eight short mysteries. A complete list can be found on her website.

Website: www.JayneOrmerod.com

CHAPTER ONE

I don't want to sound overly dramatic, but today was the day that would make or break me. As the sole proprietor of Ruff Day Doggie Boutique, I'd planned a huge marketing event. And if my big event didn't go off as hoped/anticipated/prayed for, I'd be back slinging hash on the five-a.m. shift at Breakfast at Stephanie's. Let me tell you, I am *not* a morning person. And Mr. Belvedere, my one hundred and forty-five-pound Great Dane, is *not* a morning dog. Life had been so much better since I'd become my own boss. Well, maybe not better financially, but in every other way.

All the MBAs out there would shake their heads when they heard I'd blown an entire year's marketing budget on a single event. Not a good business move, I know. I'd told myself that a thousand times.

Standing by the Chewy Vitton stuffed dog display near the front door of my shop, I gnawed a hangnail on my thumb and counted the oh-so-many things could go wrong today. I'm usually a goblet-half-full kind of person, but today the danged glass looked darned near empty.

"Darby Agnes Moore!"

I whipped my bloody thumb behind my back and turned to face the source of the accusing voice. Tianna Platt. My best friend since third grade. She stood in the doorway of my shop, dressed in her usual getup of white t-shirt, black jeans and black Sketchers boots. Her facial expression was one of complete and total irritation. Not unusual for a type-AAA perfectionist. She said the

3

people in her world constantly disappointed her. No doubt my name ranked high on that list.

Tianna crossed her arms over her tiny waist and glared at me. "Where in God's name are your pants?"

I looked down and sure enough, my fish-belly-white thighs and knobby knees jutted out from beneath my favorite New Leash on Life t-shirt. Just goes to show that mountainous amounts of stress can make one forgetful. "Oops," I said tugging my shirt down to cover the important parts, lest anyone walking down the sidewalk peeked in the large storefront window and see me half-naked. "I started to change but then remembered I needed to add more items to my list." I nodded toward a clipboard sitting atop a display of yak-milk treats. The clipboard had been Tianna's idea to help me get more organized, so it's kind of her fault I was pantless. She is the most orderly person in the world. I, on the other hand, am not. But I'm trying. Hence the clipboard.

Mr. Belvedere, my silver Great Dane, lumbered out from the back of the shop to see the source of all the commotion. He spotted Tianna, one of his favorite people, and picked up the pace.

Mr. B was tall, even by Great Dane standards, and Tianna was short, even by human standards. They stood eye-to-eye while she rubbed his jowls. "Go get some pants on," she said to me while gazing into Mr. B's baby browns. "I'll take over the list. We're running three minutes late already."

Yeah, she's so structured she schedules her life in one-minute increments.

I snapped off a salute and trotted toward the back of the store.

To clarify, I had not left my home without any pants on. I'm not that addlebrained. But how could I resist the box of oh-so-cute dog-bone-print leggings the UPS man had dropped off late yesterday afternoon? Perfect attire for today's event. I'd slipped out of my toothpick jeans, and then I remembered I needed to add a few Stop-the-Slop watering bowls to my stash of supplies. And a few colorful leashes to hang by the door of my custom dog house which would be on display for the world—or at least the residents and tourists to our sleepy bayside town—to see. Before the idea disappeared from my mind, I'd raced to find my list, so I could add the items. It took a few minutes, but I located my clipboard right where I'd left it, on the dog-treats display. Which is where Tianna had found me.

"Hey, Darbs," Tianna called to me. "Mr. B says he needs to go out. I'll walk. You start loading your stuff in the truck."

"Sounds like a plan," I hollered back.

Now fully dressed and presentable, I marched out to the front of the store. My heart swelled with pride, as it always did, when I walked in and saw all the items on display.

I can't lose all this. I just can't. Please, please, please let today go off without a hitch.

CHAPTER TWO

This grand make-me-or-break-me marketing plan had been cogitating in my head for about two years, before I ever became sole proprietor of Ruff Day. It began with a discussion with Tianna's boyfriend, an architect. Giving credit where credit is due, something he said had sparked this brilliant idea. It was so simple. I can't believe I hadn't thought of it on my own.

Here it is: if posh people can create custom homes for themselves, why can't the perfect dog house be designed for the pampered pooch? I know. Brilliant.

And even more brilliant is the name: Bark-itecture. Ha ha. Sometimes I crack myself up.

I'd begged, borrowed, and promised my first-born son in order to swing the financing to purchase Ruff Day from the owner ready to retire. As of a year ago, the shop was officially mine...and the banks. At that point, the Bark-itecture planning ramped up. I'd reached out to a few dozen civic and animal-related entities and invited them to design and build the best, most creative dog house their brains could noodle up. Every single one jumped on the idea. The local SPCA partnered with me, agreeing to supply volunteers for the event. This was gonna be the biggest thing to happen to Bay Vista in decades. And the best thing to happen to shelter dogs. And me, too, I hoped.

Today all twenty uber-creative houses were set up at the fairgrounds. The public had been invited to bring their dogs to this one day only event, try out the homes, and vote on their favorite. Today is the viewing day. Next Saturday evening, the

SPCA will hold a gala, and we will auction off the homes. All the proceeds will benefit our local animal shelter. I have branded every bit of advertising, both print and social media, to #RuffDay. Talk about win/win/win.

But only if I got the truck loaded and out to the fairgrounds. I put my rear in gear, and by the time Tianna and Mr. B returned, I'd loaded twenty gallons of water, twelve dozen organic dog-house shaped dog treats, two hundred Scoop the Poop disposable bags branded to Ruff Day Doggie Boutique, a banquet table, three chairs, and seven crates of assorted display items into the back of Tianna's black Ford F-250. It's nice to have friends with big trucks on days like this. I would have had to make three or four trips in my VW bug. And yes, when Mr. B rides shotgun in my little bug, people point and stare. What can I say? I had the car before the dog, and I can't afford a new one right now.

With Mr. Belvedere settled in his bed in my office—don't worry, he won't be alone for long as Ginger, my part-time employee, was scheduled to arrive in an hour—Tianna and I headed out to greet the day. The event wouldn't officially open until nine, but I needed to get there by seven to get things set up. The dog houses had been placed yesterday, along with a dozen food trucks, Tianna's Jamaican Jubilee included. They lined up around the edge of the parking lot in some sort of culinary campground. I hoped she would benefit from today's event as much as I did.

"Relax," Tianna said as she steered toward my little Bark-itecture creation. "The weather is great. The article in the *Bay Vista Sentinel* shone a Klieg light on the event. Even if something awful happens, you will benefit. Like they say, there's no such thing as bad publicity."

Yeah, nice words, but they did nothing to ease the discomfort of a gazillion butterflies trying to battle their way out of my stomach.

Tianna steered her truck down the fairgrounds service road, past nineteen dog houses of various shapes, sizes and levels of eccentricity. I'd spaced them every twenty feet so the display stretched out longer than a football field. For myself, I'd chosen the last spot before the service road disappeared into the woods, saving the best for last, at least in my opinion.

We bumped along, and there, at the end of the path, stood my creation, glimmering in the early morning sun. The backdrop of stately pine trees added to the bucolic setting.

I laid a hand to my throat and smiled, choking back tears of pride. I'd done it. I'd really done it. Took a dream and made it come true.

Inspired by Who-ville in *The Grinch who Stole Christmas*, the five-foot-tall structure had a dramatic and misshapen roof cascading from the apex until it almost met with the ground. A crooked smoke stack reached into the sky. A small covered front porch offered the pampered pooch a shady spot from which to watch the squirrels and birds. Painted in bright colors and crazy patterns, the dog house was, in a word, whimsical. It would bring joy to all who looked at it.

Except for this morning. A pair of shoes lay scattered on the front porch. Fancy high heels, lying on their sides, displaying shiny, blood-red soles.

Tianna stopped the truck and we both stared, mouths agape, at the scene. For it wasn't just a pair of abandoned shoes, but shoes filled with feet and attached to bare legs which disappeared into the darkness of the dog house.

"Looks like someone crashed at your dog pad." Tianna opened the truck door.

I scrambled for my door latch and followed her as she marched toward my fanciful creation. I knew what she was thinking. "This is not on the schedule."

"Let's wake her up and haul her ass…" Tianna's voice trailed off. She bent down and peered inside the dog house.

Something was off. Really off. I could feel it in my heart. No matter how hard I tried, I couldn't make my feet carry me any closer. "What?" I whispered from a safe distance.

"Um, well, the thing is, ah, well, she's naked."

Hmmm. A naked woman except for her designer heels, asleep in my dog house. This did not bode well for the start of my big event. I drew deep, calming breaths. In through the nose, out through the mouth.

"And, there's something else." Tianna cleared her voice.

Silence. Long, drawn out, painful silence.

"What!" I yelled. "Just tell me."

"It is my very unprofessional opinion that the naked woman is dead."

CHAPTER THREE

Tianna and I sat in her truck, windows up and doors locked, waiting for the police to arrive. Neither of us spoke. Seriously, what was there to say? Tianna's Pollyanna take on the pre-event publicity I'd already garnered wouldn't be enough to keep me afloat. I would be out of business by the end of the month.

I refused to give in to the tears that fizzled behind my eyes. Crying wouldn't help.

Nothing would help.

And so we sat in silence, the two of us in a stuffy truck, me picking at some invisible lint on my new leggings and Tianna tapping out a beat against the steering wheel with her thumbs. An odd, frenetic beat that escalated my twitchiness. More than escalated, sent it soaring off the flippin' charts.

What did Tianna have to brood about? I mean, it wasn't her business that was about to crash and burn. It was mine.

And then it hit me. Tianna had seen the dead woman, up close and way too personal. I hadn't even asked. Some best friend I am.

I reached out and laid my hand on hers, until that one, at least, stopped tapping its staccato beat. "Oh, honey. You okay?"

"Yup."

"Wanna talk about it?"

"Nope."

Silence. A heavy, gloomy silence that stretched out until broken by the flashing red and blue lights of a police cruiser. Yeah. Help had arrived. I practically fell out of the truck in my haste to get out. I'd had enough sitting in the truck with all that tension practically suffocating me.

I waved my arms like a maniac to make it clear we were the ones who made the call. Yes, I know there was no one else around, but this is how I've seen it done in the movies. It's some sort of universal language for "I'm the damsel in distress."

The vehicle stopped a few feet behind the truck. A tall, tan, sunglass-wearing officer emerged from his low-slung sedan. He tugged on black sterile gloves as he walked my direction. His swagger may or may not have been caused by all the threatening items hanging from his utility belt.

"Thank God you're here," I said. "That poor woman…" I pointed toward my doghouse.

"Your name, please?" he asked.

"Darby Agnes Moore, but most people just call me Darbs."

"Thank you, Miss Moore. Can you tell me what happened?"

I summarized the events to the best of my ability, which came out a bit garbled because, well, truth be told, I was feeling a bit garbled. Something about that uniform. More about being up close and personal with that gun on his hip that his fingers rested against.

"Do you know the identity of the victim?"

I pulled my gaze away from the menacing weapon and looked into the officer's mirrored sunglasses. "Um, no. I didn't actually see it. I mean her. "

"How do you know it's a female?"

"I could see the high heel and long legs from where I stood. Definitely lady legs. Her head and torso were inside the doghouse, so I couldn't see them. Tianna, my friend, is the one who peeked inside and told me she was naked, except for the shoes."

A smirk appeared at the corner of his mouth. "How do you know she's dead?"

"Tianna told me. I don't know how she knows. I didn't ask." Yeah, in my selfishness of the event's success, I hadn't asked a lot of things. Had it been a gruesome scene? Of course it had. I should have offered emotional support.

"And where is Tianna now?"

"Sitting in her truck." I pointed toward the drivers' side of Tianna's black F-250. "I think she's still processing it all."

Another police cruiser pulled up, lights flashing. It rolled to a stop a few inches from where we stood. "Watcha got, Rawlins?" The woman in the police cruiser also wore mirrored sunglasses. They must be standard issue. Along with the uniform. The only difference between the two was the female officer's thick, ash-blond hair was pulled into a tight ponytail. I didn't envy her that. Tight ponytails always gave me a headache.

"Hey, Jurkowski," Rawlins said in a friendly way that belied the scowl on his face. "I've got a statement from Miss Moore, here." He hitched his head in my direction. "You get a statement from the one in the truck. She found the body. I'll go check out the crime scene. Don't let them compare stories," he warned before sauntering down the service road toward my dog house.

I didn't like the sound of that. I mean, he didn't...couldn't possibly...think *we* had killed the woman. Oh, lord. This day was going from bad to worst-day-ever.

Jurkowski got out of her cruiser and flashed me a Mona Lisa smile. She was all business. They must teach that attitude at the police academy because I'd never met anyone outside of law enforcement who had such a cool-as-a-snow-cone personality.

I settled my rear end on the back bumper of Tianna's truck and nibbled on my nails. I mean, what else could I do?

Tianna and Jurkowski spoke in tones so low I couldn't overhear. And yes, I will admit that I tried, but the cacophony of chirping birds on this glorious early summer morning made that impossible.

Another vehicle approached, this one a crime scene van. Two men jumped out and began cordoning off the area surrounding my dog house with bright yellow crime-scene tape. It totally ruined the Whoville vibe of my Bark-itecture creation, let me tell you! I wanted to go rip it down, but remembering Rawlins' gun, I suppressed the urge.

Another car pulled up, this one unmarked, but I wasn't fooled. The lightbar in the back window gave it away. A tall man emerged from the vehicle, dressed for the boardroom, not a day at the fairgrounds. He sported the same mirrored sunglasses as the other two police officers, which he removed as he surveyed the scene. Same all-business expression as Rawlins and Jurkowski. Had to be an attitude they taught at the academy.

The well-dressed man—a detective, I surmised—consulted briefly with Rawlins before slowly walking the crime scene area, looking for whatever itty-bitty bit of evidence he could find. Just like I'd seen in the movies.

The truck door opened. I turned as Tianna emerged from her seat. No sign of Jurkowski.

"Come on," Tianna said in her I'm-in-a-bitchy-mood-don't-mess-with-me voice which I'd come to know and love over the two decades we'd been friends. Well, almost two-decades…there was that brief interruption during college when we'd lost touch. Tianna called that her lost year. I'd never asked, and she'd never told.

"Let's get the truck unloaded," she said. "There's plenty of room to set up without disturbing the crime scene." She started pulling things onto the truck's lowered tailgate.

I walked over to help. "Yeah, like you know anything about not disturbing a crime scene." I laughed. I mean seriously. Tianna had to be the most law-abiding citizen ever.

Tianna didn't laugh with me. Instead, her face was quite serious. Deadly serious. Wait. That sounded wrong on so many levels considering there was a body lying not more than thirty feet from us. Let's say abso-effing-lutely serious.

She grabbed one end of a folding table and motioned for me to grab the other. We carried it to a spot within arm's reach of a police car. Too close for comfort, in my book. But on the plus side, it was in sight of my darling little dog house, enabling me to keep an eye on all the goings on.

We worked in silence as we unloaded the rest of the items from the truck, each lost in our own thoughts. But I got to the point where I couldn't stand her sullenness any more. Inquiring minds wanted to know the details of what she'd seen in my doghouse. Rawlins had spiked my curiosity. How had Tianna known the body was dead? I hadn't seen her bend down to check for a pulse or anything.

"Was it gruesome?" I asked.

She paused flipping through the stack of Ruff Day Doggie Boutique postcards she'd been about to set on the table. "Yeah. Death by nail gun. Had to be fifty nails imbedded in her. Head. Breasts. Stomach. Left butt cheek." She tapped the stack of cards on the table, straightening them into a neat 4x6 stack of glossy promotional material.

My mental image of the sight was, possibly, worse than the actual scene. I have a vivid imagination. Vomit gurgled at the back of my throat. I turned my head to avoid spewing my graham-cracker breakfast all over my table of freebies. Once the feeling passed, I hazarded a glance at her. "A lot of blood?"

She nodded.

There was something else, something she wasn't telling me. "There's more, isn't there?"

Tianna nodded. When she spoke, her voice was barely above a whisper. "I recognized her. Despite the nails poking from her face... Oh gawd, I recognized her."

I gasped. "Was it someone we know?"

This time she shook her head. "Not we. I. She went to college with Hayden."

Hayden Burnside was Tianna's Mr. Right Now, with the potential for being Mr. Right Forever. The only thing holding that back was him. He didn't seem ready to settle down, while Tianna's biological clock clicked like a runaway freight train heading downhill. That was only one issue they needed to work through, though. I also found him a wee bit too possessive for my liking.

"We met at a party a few weeks ago." Tianna spoke to the ground, not me. "She exuded the slut aroma, so finding her wearing nothing but the latest eight-hundred-dollar Louboutins was not a surprise."

I let that all sink in. But it didn't set well.

"She'd moved to Bay Vista a few months ago. Some kind of new job. I don't remember the details."

Bay Vista was a small seaside town on the Albemarle Sound, relying more on tourist dollars than big industry to keep the economy going. And neither one supported an $800-pair-of-shoes lifestyle. That's more big city kinda stuff. So, what would bring the woman here? Many questions swirled in my mind. But one took front and center, and flashed like a neon light...had the dead woman moved to Bay Vista to rekindle an old flame? I cleared my throat before speaking. "Did she and Hayden have a, ah..." how to phrase this delicately? "A history?" I looked Tianna straight in her downcast eyes.

Her lips pressed together in a thin grim line. She didn't trust herself to speak.

I didn't trust myself to speak either, because the thought that popped into my head was the most terrifying thing...isn't the jealous girlfriend the police's prime suspect?

She must have sensed my steely gaze upon her. "Don't look at me. I didn't kill her."

CHAPTER FOUR

Tianna left to tend to her food truck. She promised to bring me something to eat once the lunch rush was over, giving me too much time to ponder the six-million-dollar question...If Tianna hadn't killed the girl with no name, who had?

I sat in my chair while the police took photos. A lot of photos. I mean, how many photos of a naked woman did a person need? Never mind. Forget I said that.

I will admit to snapping a few photos of my own. Surreptitiously, of course. I needed to capture the Bark-itecture that wasn't. I could use them to support my case to the bank when the loans came due. Maybe they would take sympathy upon me, realizing the disaster was not of my own making. I'm still a darn good business woman! Who loved dogs! I would forgive me a missed payment—or three—wouldn't you?

I peeked down the service road at the other nineteen dog houses. People and their pets were slowly making their way towards me. Not the crowds I had hoped for, but still, people and pets. And they all were having fun exploring the dog houses. That warmed the cockles of my heart. But, at this rate, it would be another thirty minutes or longer before they got to me.

I straightened the merchandise. I double checked the water bowls. I stacked and restacked the scoop the poop bags.

And most annoyingly of all, I had on constant mental loop the question of the dead woman's identity, and that of her killer. I mean, how could I not think about that?

The first attendee arrived at my site. A young woman in a

turquoise midriff tee, short white shorts and flip flops. I'd seen her coming, bypassing all the other dog houses and beelining it straight for me. Perhaps lured by the gaggle of police vehicles?

"What a great event," she said as she approached my table. "Can I get a picture of you in the foreground?"

She looked so hopeful, how could I refuse? I held up a Ruff Day Doggie Boutique sign in front of me while striking a pose. My dog house, wrapped in crime scene tape, featured prominently in the background.

"Do you know what happened?" she asked, her thumbs poised above her cell phone screen. "I want to caption the photo."

"We found a dead woman in my dog house this morning." No such thing as bad publicity, I reminded myself.

Her face filled with glee while her thumbs frenetically tapped out a message.

"A naked dead woman," I added, unable to resist adding that salacious detail.

The young woman squealed with glee. I mean squealed! She stared at the screen for a few minutes, then flashed me her phone. "Look! My snap is going viral," she said.

Viral was good.

And it garnered a steady parade of looky-loos and morbid curiosity seekers throughout the rest of the morning. I posed when asked; talked up Ruff Day whenever anyone would listen; accepted the compliments on my doghouse; and patiently answered questions regarding the police activity being carried out behind me. If questioned, I would claim the event a success, on every level. Except one—the dead woman in my dog house. And that was kind of a biggie. I'd sort that guilt out later.

My stomach began its low, hungry gurgle. Lunchtime. Way past lunch time. When I glanced at my cellphone, I was surprised to see it was three-fifteen. The day had passed quickly. Where was Tianna? My mouth watered for one of the Jamaican Jubilee's jerk chicken sammies with a side of pineapple coleslaw, all washed down with an ice-cold sweet tea. She makes the best sweet tea this side of the Rockies.

As if she'd read my mind (and yeah, that happens a lot) her diminutive figure hurried my way, carrying the familiar green, gold, and black patterned take-out bag.

"You saved my life," I said as she handed me the bag. I opened it up and took a long sniff of the spicy jerk chicken. Nirvana. "Can you watch the table while I scarf this down?"

"Sure thing." She grabbed a stack of postcards and began working her way through the crowd. Tianna had missed her calling. I swear, she could sell tequila to a teetotaler.

I couldn't wander far, what with the crime-scene tape and all, so I parked myself at the perimeter and dug in. Why does food always taste better when someone else cooks it?

There wasn't much going on around my dog house. The body had been removed about an hour ago and the looky-loos along with it. Only Rawlins and the detective still hung around, chatting and gesturing.

Rawlins spotted me, took a good long look at my lunch, and in a dozen long, purposeful strides he stood before me. He whipped off his sunglasses and glared at me. "Where did you get that?"

"What, my lunch? It's jerk chicken from one of the food trucks. You want a bite? It's delicious."

"No, I do not want a bite. I want to know which food truck."

"The Jamaican Jubilee. It's owned by my friend Tianna. You remember her, from this morning?"

"The suspect who found the body?"

"Suspect?" I put my hand to my throat. "Since when did Tianna become an official suspect?"

"Since we found one of her food wrappers in the victim's hand. Your friend has some explaining to do."

I turned and searched for Tianna in the crowd. But she wasn't there. Nope. My best friend was scampering as fast as her little legs would carry her away from the crime scene.

"Mullins, we got a runner," Rawlins called over his shoulder and then took off at a fast clip down the service road.

Tianna didn't stand a chance.

CHAPTER FIVE

Tianna slid into the booth across from me. We had a standing date at Breakfast at Stephanie's every Monday morning at eight a.m. It's our wind down from a busy work weekend. I hadn't expected her to show today, considering the last time I'd seen her she was beatin' feet down the fairgrounds access road with Officer Rawlins in hot pursuit. Add to that she'd gone radio silent, not responding to the ga-zillion texts I'd shot off last night.

"You're here," I said, stating the obvious.

Tianna let the menu slip out of her hands and slide across the table. "Where else would I be?" she asked.

I slouched against the back of my seat. "My money was on Rawlins yesterday. No offense, but that man could run."

"Yeah, he could."

"I figured he'd caught you and thrown you in the pokey."

"I already told you. I did not kill that woman." Statement said through clenched teeth.

"I believe you." I sat up reached across the table and squeezed her arm. "I don't think Rawlins believes you, though."

"Yeah. Nobody believes a chick with a record."

Ah, another allusion to the lost year. But that was a discussion to be had over a bottle...or three...of wine, not pancakes and java.

Stephanie herself appeared at our table, carrying two mugs of fragrant coffee. "Y'all heard about that dead woman out to the fairgrounds?" She placed a mug in front of each of us.

"Heard about it," I said. "Tianna here found it—I mean

21

her—in my dog house at Bark-itecture."

"Get out of town!" Stephanie shooed Tianna further into the booth and squeezed in. Stephanie leaned in real close, and crooked her finger for us to lean in close, too. "You know her roommate works here, right?"

"I don't even know the dead woman's name," I said, sliding a no-thanks-to-you look towards Tianna.

"Monique Mallicott," Stephanie offered. "Her roommate is my new waitress." She hitched her head to her right. "Brittany Grant."

Tianna and I snuck a peak. Not exactly a furtive one, though. In fact, we couldn't have been more obvious if we'd tried.

Two tables away stood a petite blond woman dressed in traditional Breakfast at Stephanie's waitress attire. In a nod to the quintessential romantic comedy *Breakfast at Tiffany's*, all staff sported a Tiffany-blue golf shirt, white pants and white Keds. Blue hairbow optional. Brittney sported one. I, on the other hand, am not a hairbow kind of girl so had never worn one during my waitressing career.

Stephanie slapped us both on the arm. "Don't look, or she'll think we're talking about her."

Tianna rolled her eyes. "We *are* talking about her."

"She's new, isn't she?" I asked.

"Hired her two weeks ago. Works hard, gotta give her that."

"Where did she come from?"

"Somewhere inland. Raleigh, maybe? Moved into her aunt's house. A big ol' Victorian at the north end of the bay. Renting out rooms to help cover the costs."

"Where's the aunt?" Tianna asked.

"In a memory care unit up Norfolk way."

I stretched my eyes to the side, as far as they would go and took a long look. Brittany delivered a plate of double-decker egg and cheese sandwiches to the table beside us. Service with a smile. As if she didn't have a care in the world. My last roommate experience was over a decade ago, my junior year of college, but I have to think I wouldn't be smiling the next day if my roommate had been brutally murdered. "Seems chipper." I sipped my coffee, then added another cream.

Tianna poured three sugars in her coffee and gave it a stir. Her eyes, though, were checking Brittney out, too. "Too chipper, if you ask me."

I shrugged off Tianna's observation. "It's not a crime to be chipper."

"It is on a Monday morning." Tianna took a sip of her coffee and grimaced. Not sweet enough, I didn't imagine. Tianna liked coffee with her morning sugar.

Stephanie glanced over her shoulder and then back at us. "Like I said, a hard worker, always smiling, super nice to the customers. But boy, oh boy, we witnessed another side of her when her roommate, that dead woman, came by last Friday. Seems there was no love lost between them. They had a knock-down drag-out right here during the lunch rush hour. Brittney screamed, 'I'm gonna kill you, you son of a biscuit maker.' Actually, she used another word for biscuit maker, but this here's a family-friendly restaurant." Stephanie shifted in her seat. "Anyway, Monique hopped on her moped and roared away."

"Motive," Tianna said. "And probably opportunity. Now we need to find the means." She tapped her finger against the table.

What in the world was Tianna doing, going all James Rockford on me? Roommates fight all the time. And how many times had I threatened to kill someone? It's a commonly accepted figure of speech. Nobody means it.

I caught a flash of blue out of the corner of my eye. "Hush now. Here she comes."

The petite blond sidled up to our table. Brittany was older than I expected, though, judging by the lifelines around her eyes. Maybe early thirties? Late to the post-secondary-education party.

"Miss Stephanie," Brittany said. "Someone is asking to see the manager. Up at the register."

"What now?" Stephanie pasted a fake smile on her face and hauled herself out of her seat. "Brittany, can you take care of these folks for me, please?" Off she hustled.

Brittany took a pad of paper out of her apron pocket. She smiled as if she didn't have a care in the world. Maybe she didn't.

But maybe she did. Call it a gut feeling. Although my gut feelings only pan out about fifty percent of the time, so that doesn't prove a thing.

"What can I get for you ladies today?" she asked.

I placed my standard order of blueberry pancakes buried under a mountain of fresh whipped cream, two eggs lightly scrambled and three slices of crisp bacon. I waited for Tianna to do the same. It's a tradition to start our week off with our pancake breakfast, ever since Tianna hit the lottery for ten grand one Monday the same day Ruff Day Doggie Boutique came up for sale, and I was under contract by supper time. We considered it our good-luck breakfast. And it had served us well. At least until last week.

"I'll have the Stephanie Special, eggs over easy, sourdough toast, and burn it, please," Tianna said.

What? Had I heard correctly? That did not bode well for the week ahead. A bad feeling filled my stomach. You know, the cement-ball-in-the-gut kinda feeling.

Tianna pressed the menu to Brittany's outstretched hand. "Hey, what happened to your thumb?"

Brittany held out her left thumb. The nail was black as all get out, and the skin around it was angry red. "Learned a lesson last week. Don't ever try to hang a curtain rod after a night of Tequila Sunrises! I put a nail right through my thumb. Hurt like a son of a bitch!"

Holy schnikes!

She gave her hand a shake, then tucked her thumb inside her fingers. The smile reappeared on her lips. "I'll get these orders in right away."

Once she was out of earshot, I settled back into my seat. "Well, well, Miss Nancy Drew. I think you found us our first suspect."

"Second suspect." Tianna stirred her coffee and then licked the spoon . "You forgot I'm the first.

CHAPTER SIX

I polished off the delicious breakfast, scraping up the last bits of maple syrup with my last bite of buttery blueberry pancake. I threw in my napkin, leaned back in my seat and rubbed my full belly. A satisfied smile crept across my face.

A shadow fell across our table. I looked up. My eyes stopped when they got to the gun. Safely holstered on a police utility belt, but it sent my heart a-thumpin' as if the barrel was pointed right between my eyes just the same.

"Ladies, may I have a word?" Female voice. Not one I recognized. "You might remember me from yesterday at the fairgrounds," the gun-owner said. "Meg Jurkowski, Bay Vista PD."

It took great effort, but I dragged my gaze up to her face. Yup, same ponytailed police officer from the fairgrounds who had pulled up and joined Rawlins for the preliminary investigation.

She pulled off her mirrored aviator glasses and I got a good look at her stormy blue eyes.

"Please join us." I mean, what else do you say to a woman with a gun? I scooted along my booth seat so that she could sit.

Her police utility belt made subtle protests as she slid on the bench next to me. Less than three inches separated me from the holstered gun and other implements of suspect-catching. Kind of a creepy feeling.

Brittany brought Jurkowski a glass of Coke. The police officer made a big show of unwrapping her straw, dipping it into the drink and stirring, stirring, stirring. All without uttering a single word. It's an old police trick I'd seen on TV a gazillion times…let the suspect fill the conversational abyss.

I watched Tianna, who watched Jurkowski's movements with great interest. The tension rose with every swish of the straw.

Tianna cleared her throat. "Got any suspects in the Mallicott murder?"

Jurkowski twisted in her seat, a slight smile curling at the corner of her mouth. She bent her head until her mouth met the straw and took a long drink. When finished, she sat back and let out a satisfied sigh. "The only thing I've heard is time of death is three a.m., give or take an hour. But holy hell, what a way to go, huh?" She sipped more Coke.

I tried not to picture a woman with over fifty nails thrust into her various body parts, but was unsuccessful. Be still my queasy stomach!

"Too early for the tox report, I imagine," Tianna said.

"Yeah, that's gonna take a few days."

Tianna fidgeted in her seat, a sure sign she was waging an internal battle about saying something versus keeping her big yap shut. "I didn't tell you everything yesterday," Tianna whispered.

Do I know my BFF or what?

Jurkowski leaned back in her seat, all casual like, as if Tianna had asked her opinion about the chances of the Nationals making it to the playoffs this year. She rested one arm on the table while the other one stretched along the back of the bench seat, her fingertips almost brushing my shoulder. "Want to tell me now?" she asked, ever so casually.

A frisson of trepidation zapped through my entire body.

Tianna ran her fingers through her hair, scrubbed her face, and said, "Yeah. Okay." She then proceeded to share the details of her acquaintance with Monique Mallicott, how they'd met at a party a few weeks ago, and how the victim just happened to show up in Bay Vista, intent on rekindling a relationship with Tianna's boyfriend, Hayden.

"That confirms what Monique's roommate told us."

"Brittany?"

"No, a girl by the name of Angela. Any idea what this great job was?" Jurkowski asked.

"That's just it. There was no job. I confronted Hayden last night and he admitted that Monique had been stalking him on Facebook for the past few months. They had a thing back in the day, but Hayden said it was all in the past. She told him she loved the pictures he posted of our bayside community, so one day she packed up her things and drove here."

"When?"

"First I saw of her was three weeks ago." Tianna shrugged. "She may have been here longer. Did you ask Brittany? The other roommate? She's new to the community, too. Started working here two weeks ago."

"Hmmm." I dabbed my napkin on a splot of maple syrup on the table. "Quite a coincidence."

Jurkowski sat up straight in her seat. "There are two things I don't believe in. Unicorns and coincidences." Her gaze scanned the room. "Is Brittany working today? I'd like to talk to her."

Tianna turned in her seat. "I don't see her. Maybe she's in the back."

Stephanie stopped by our table to refill coffee mugs. "Can I get you a refill, Officer?"

"No, thanks. Gotta cut myself off. It's shaping up to be one of those days where bathroom breaks are few and far between."

Stephanie nodded as if she heard that a lot. "Can I get you anything else?"

Jurkowski ran her thumb across her lower lip. "Maybe a few answers?"

"Absolutely." Stephanie slipped in the seat beside Tianna. "What can I help you with?"

"Your new waitress. Brittany. What can you tell me about her?"

"She's a damn hard worker," Stephanie said. "I wish I had a dozen like her. But I don't imagine you're interested in her work ethic."

Jurkowski shook her head. "Tell me what you know about

her background, where she came from, and if you know anything about her relationship with Monique Mallicott."

Stephanie shot a questioning glance to me and then to Tianna, who nodded for her to proceed.

I leaned back in my seat, trying to relax when in fact inside I was a jumble of nerves. I had never sat in on an actual police inquiry. There was an electricity in the air that I couldn't describe. We were on the precipice of a clue that would break the case wide open. I knew it! Reality TV had nothing on this. I rubbed my hands together in anticipation.

Stephanie summarized the employment application, adding a few more details, the kind of which would have come up in polite conversation while rolling hundreds of sets of cutlery into napkins every day, a task I'd dreaded for its monotony but built the most intimate sense of camaraderie with my fellow waitresses. We'd had some pretty deep discussions, solved some of the world's problems, and cultivated some lifelong friends. If you want to get to know a person, roll cutlery with them.

Brittany Grant's story in a nutshell: graduated from NC State, hadn't been able to find a job in her field of sociology; offered to move into her aunt's neglected cottage along the bay and make the repairs in exchange for a portion of the proceeds when it sold; planned to use that money to further her education as a social worker; the house-flipping process was slower and more expensive than she'd anticipated so picked up two roommates from a Craig's List post; Angela was great; Monique was super messy and behind on her weekly rent; Brittany had told her she needed to move out, resulting in the big showdown at the diner on Friday.

Tianna took a sip of her sugar-slash-coffee and set the mug on the table. Her mind was working at Mach speed again, I could tell.

"Is Brittany here now, so I can ask her a few questions?" Jurkowski asked.

Stephane shook her head. "Today is her regular day off, but she came in to cover while Jillian rushed her dog to the vet."

I placed my hand over my heart. "I hope Zuzu's okay."

"Had a run-in with a cat. Scratched cornea. Got some ointment. She'll be fine. Anyway, Brittany left about ten minutes ago."

Jurkowski started to get up from her seat.

Tianna slowed Jurkowski by laying a hand on her wrist. "Wait a sec." Tianna worried her lower lip before speaking to Stephanie. "Is Brittany doing the renovations herself, or is she hiring subcontractors?"

"She's doing as much as she can herself," Stephanie answered. "She plans to hire electricians and carpenters when she gets to that point. Right now, she's adding and removing a few walls to open up the living area."

"What do you think the chances are her toolbox includes a nail gun?"

Pretty good, if you ask me. But nobody asked me.

Before anyone else could answer, a commotion erupted at the front of the diner.

A twenty-something blond woman raced to our table and confronted Stephanie. "Where's Brittany?"

"She left a bit ago, why?"

"Because I got a text that our house is on fire!"

Officer Jurkowski slid out of her seat and sprinted out the front door.

I looked at Tianna. She looked at me. We telepathically exchanged the question, "Do we stay or do we go?"

Silly question.

CHAPTER SEVEN

I threw some bills on the table and Tianna and I raced out of the diner hot on the heels of Officer Jurkowski.

Two problems presented themselves. One, both Tianna and I had walked to the diner, and it would take at least fifteen minutes to get to a car; and two, we didn't have an address where Brittany lived. "Along the bay" was kind of vague, considering the town of Bay Vista stretched seven miles to the north and six miles to the south of where we currently stood.

A third problem presented itself, too. Mr. Belvedere needed to be walked and my store needed to be opened. "You go on without me," I said to Tianna. "Send me a text when you have more details."

Tianna took off at lightning speed. She sure was getting her exercise lately. At least this time, she was running toward the police instead of away from them.

A few minutes later, a black Bay Vista PD Dodge Charger careened north up Vista Boulevard, lights flashing, with Tianna riding shotgun.

My steps back to Ruff Day were brisk, spurred on by the many questions swirling in my head. Would someone really kill over being evicted? Especially having only been there a few weeks? Tiana had mentioned Monique was a little cray-cray, but murderous cray-cray? I'd never met the woman so was not in a position to judge. Not that I even knew how to judge anyone's murderous intentions in the first place. I'm a good judge of dog-character. People, not so much.

Is it even possible that a person would kill for such a small issue? I couldn't imagine it. Yet Brittany had the means and a possible motive. Ah, but did she have the opportunity? The next logical step would be to see if she had an alibi for Friday night. Good thing we had a Cracker Jack police force. They'd know the answer to that by lunchtime.

Mr. Belvedere met me at the shop's door. My heart melted every time I laid eyes on my big boy. He gave me a quick ice-cream-cone lick up the side of my face. I kissed him back on the top of his head and snapped on his leash. As soon as I opened the door, he took off for the park, me along for the ride. Fortunately, I managed to stay on my feet, which isn't always the case when Mr. Belvedere decides to run.

He checked his Pee-mail (and there was a lot to sniff this morning!) tussled with a few friends, and finally completed his business. We raced back to the shop in time to flip the closed sign to open and turn on the Carolina Beach Music channel on my streaming audio system, the soundtrack of my life since moving to Bay Vista six years ago. *I... wanna soak up the sun...*

Two women walked in at the same time, and although they looked to be about the same age—mid sixties—I don't think they were together. The customer dressed head-to-toe in Talbot's latest fashion beelined it straight for what amounts to the chips and pretzels aisle for dogs. The other more casually (and in my opinion, more comfortably) dressed woman dawdled by the clearance rack.

Mr. Belvedere, now settled in his plush bed, lifted his head and looked around for canine customers. There were none. He put his head down and went back to sleep.

"May I help you?" I asked no one in particular.

Casual customer shook her head as she browsed through the dog-kerchiefs in various sizes and colors. I'd hoped they'd be big sellers but turned out to be duds. I couldn't give the dang things away.

"Just looking," she said.

"Yes," the woman pawing through the doggie junk snacks said. "My little Poppy has had two horrible experiences over the past week, and I'm looking for a little something to lift her spirits."

"Oh, no," casual customer said. "What happened, if you don't mind me asking?"

Poppy's mom shuddered, as if the mere thought of what her poor dog went through was too disturbing to talk about. But at the same time, she seemed eager to share the gory details of her pup's harrowing experiences. "A week ago, my husband and I tripped up to Newport, Rhode Island for a little getaway. We were married there, so we make a trip up every anniversary. Anyway, our usual dog sitter cancelled at the last minute, so my husband recruited one of his new employees to come stay at the house." The woman's voice shook as she spoke, taking on a higher pitch with each sentence. "Only when we returned home, Poppy was all alone. No sign of the sitter. And she was being paid to be there twenty-four-seven. My little Poppy hadn't been brushed, water bowl empty, and I don't think she'd been outside for a good long time. No accidents, mind you, my Poppy wouldn't do that. But she chewed up one of my coffee tables, a sure sign of emotional distress."

I offered a *tsk-tsk* of sympathy.

Casual customer had her hands on her hips as if looking to start a fight with the AWOL dog sitter. "I hope that woman was on life support at the hospital! There is no other excuse to leave any animal without water!"

Poppy's mom lifted her designer purse—maybe Kate Spade, maybe a knock-off, I'm not a handbag connoisseur—higher on her shoulder. "You said it, sister. She claims she had a medical emergency and was only away for a little bit while she went to pick up a prescription. I don't believe it. My neighbors reported not seeing her car there overnight. Imagine my poor little Poppy having to sleep alone. That woman was a liar. And a thief! She stole my husband's loose change, too. Probably not more than a hundred dollars, but seriously. Just goes to show you can't trust anyone anymore. I was so mad I practically killed the woman. My husband had to pull me off her."

"What was her name? I work for the SPCA, and I can spread

the word for people not to use her."

"Monique something."

"Monique Mallicott?" I asked. No! What were the odds?

"Yes, that's it. Have you dealt with her before?"

I rested my hip on the counter. How to sugarcoat the news? Never mind, there was no sugarcoating this. "She was found murdered yesterday morning."

"What?" Casual customer's voice sounded like a needle scraped across a vinyl record. "I read about that in the paper." Her mouth hung open as she shook her head in disbelief.

Poppy's mom sniffed. "Well, I say good riddance to bad rubbish."

Wow, that was a bit harsh. I glanced at casual woman and she at me. Yeah, we were thinking the same thing.

Poppy's mom pawed through a bin of bagged dog treats. "Do you have any Peanut Butter Pup Puffs? They're Poppy's favorite."

Mr. Belvedere lumbered over and stuck his nose in the bin. He knew how to find peanut butter anything. Best sales clerk I've ever had. And he works for kibble.

"What else happened to Poppy last week?" I asked. If the dog sitter had inflicted more pain and suffering to Poppy, I might have to add this customer to my suspects list. There was definitely enough venom in her voice to lead me to believe she was capable of murder.

"My Poppy has had to wear the cone of shame for a week!"

Casual customer and I commiserated on that. No dog-mom likes to have their fur baby in an Elizabethan collar. I don't imagine it's much fun for the dog, either.

Mr. Belvedere selected two packets of snacks and, holding them gently in his big mouth, carried them to the counter.

I rang up the items. "Nine dollars and sixty-five cents."

Poppy's mom dug deep into her cavernous purse and extracted a platinum Visa. She strode toward the counter.

I ran the card through my machine, surreptitiously checking the name: Emmaline G. Forrester. "I hope Poppy enjoys her treats."

"It seemed like such a tiny thing at first, but turned into a big problem. My husband was working to finish a fantastic new dog house for Poppy. It was on display at that Bark-itecture event. Maybe you saw it? Anyway, my poor baby got a nick on her paw when she got too close to my husband when he was using a nail gun."

Nail gun? My interest in this woman rocketed into outer space. That was some coincidence, wasn't it?

What had Jurkowski said about coincidences?

Oh, yeah. No such thing.

CHAPTER EIGHT

Did I Google Emmaline G. Forrester the second she left my shop? You betcha. My fingers were flying across the keys before the shop door closed behind her. I was curious by nature, and I couldn't stand not knowing the extent of the Monique-Emmaline connection.

Like many people of a certain age, Emmaline's social media presence bordered on non-existent. Her Facebook privacy setting was public but revealed little more than her birthdate (April 13, 1951) and her education (B.A. in Art History from Randolph-Macon Woman's College, Lynchburg, Virginia). The rest was blank. No posts or pictures or even any friends on her list. I'm guessing a child or grandchild had set the account up for her, and she hadn't logged on since.

A generic search revealed Emmaline to be a huge supporter of the S.P.C.A., as evidenced by the many photos of her, front-and-center, at various fund-raising events. Married for forty-plus years to Charles Forrester, a very successful litigation attorney from Raleigh. Three grown children, five grandchildren and two itty-bitty great-grands. They'd recently retired to their summer home here in Bay Vista where Charles decided to spend his reclining years as editor-in-chief of a small-press publishing business. I made a mental note to confirm Monique's employment there.

A little deeper search found their address, 4896 Bay Vista Drive. Bingo! I would drive by this afternoon.

Further Google searches failed to return any criminal

background for Ms. Emmaline. Zero. Zip. Nada. A model citizen. I couldn't even find mention of a parking ticket in the Police Blotter section of *The Bay Vista Journal*. I mean, who doesn't occasionally park a few inches over the white line? I, myself, had a stack of them.

So, Emmaline Forrester didn't look like the killing type.

I then did a little cyber stalking of Brittany Grant, our waitress from this morning. A person of interest, as the police might say. Well, maybe not the police, but Tianna and I considered her as such. Brittany was much more social-media savvy and had her privacy locked up tight. I scrolled through pages of party-girl pictures but didn't learn much more. Checking the archives of the local paper, I found a brief mention of Gertrude Grant, aka GiGi, moving to a memory care unit in Norfolk. It didn't take a member of the Prometheus Society to figure out that connection. Address for Brittany—and hence the recently deceased Monique—4824 Bay Vista Drive. Hmmm. Pretty close to Emmaline Forrester.

The coincidences kept piling up.

Mr. Belvedere picked his leash off the hanger and dropped it at my feet. Time for his mid-afternoon potty break. Subtly is not his strong suit.

I hung the BACK SOON sign on the door and off we trotted, down the quaint streets of my little seaside town. My heart swelled with pride for my dog. His regal conformation was on full display as he walked head up, ears perked, hooked tail swooshing gracefully from side to side. I'd rescued him from the SPCA two years ago. Somebody had surrendered him because he grew too big. Hello! He's a Great Dane! But one woman's toss-off is another woman's lucky day. I'd been at a low point in my life, and he brought me back to a high point. I often wondered who rescued whom.

I hummed the "Murder, She Wrote" theme song as Mr. Belvedere and I hurried along the boardwalk. He had business to take care of. I had thoughts to ponder. We had two suspects. Three, if you counted Tianna, which I did not. Both had motive...albeit a weak motive...to kill someone. Both had means, with access to a murder weapon. Now it came down to who had opportunity?

I needed to swap notes with Tianna. Why hadn't she called or texted me about the fire at Brittany's house? And, more importantly, had she found any evidence that it tied into Monique's murder?

My phone dinged an incoming text. Tianna! Finally! WHERE THE HELL ARE YOU?

I texted back WALKING MR. B. WHERE ARE YOU?

STANDING OUTSIDE RUFF DAY. LOTS TO TELL.

ME TOO. ON OUR WAY.

I dashed up Bay Vista Drive with my dog in tow. Although technically, I was the one in tow. As I've mentioned, Mr. Belvedere is a big boy, thirty-two inches at the withers, over six feet toe-to-tail, and at a modest one hundred and forty-five pounds, he weighs slightly more than me. We were going at a reasonably quick pace when he spotted Tianna standing in front of Ruff Day.

Woof woof! His deep bark echoed down the street as he transitioned into a smooth canter. Smooth, but fast. I held on for all I was worth.

A young pig-tailed girl pointed at us and yelled, "Look, mommy. A runaway pony!" Her mother yanked the child into the safety of Connie's Cards and Gifts.

A woman carrying a bakery box from Sweet Stuff screamed, dropped her box of goodies and raced across the street. Horns honked. Tires screeched. More shouts.

The noise spooked Mr. B, and he broke into an all-out gallop.

My leather sandals made a slap-slap sound against the cement as I focused all of my energy on not face-planting on the cement.

One block later, still upright but breathless, we arrived safely at Ruff Day.

Tianna pulled me in close. "Two words," Tianna stage-whispered to me. "Suspected arson."

"What?" I screeched.

Tianna made the hurry up motion while I fumbled with the key to the lock. "Inside," she said, casting a furtive glance over her shoulder.

"Why the hush-hush?" I asked. The door swung open, and Tianna shoved me through.

Mr. Belvedere snuggled up to Tianna while she rubbed his jowls. "Meg told me this in strictest confidence."

"Are you and Officer Jurkowski on friendly terms now?"

"You know the old police saying, keep your friends close, but your suspects closer."

No, I hadn't heard that, but it made sense. Especially in this situation. "Slow down, and start from the beginning. But follow me. I need to get set up for the dirty dogs scheduled for baths this afternoon." The back of my store had two bays for self-serve dog washing. Very popular with the owners who did not like to furry-up their own bathrooms. Not so popular with the dogs.

Tianna talked while I pulled out a selection of organic shampoos and fluffy towels and arranged them on the counter. "So, it seems that both Brittany and the other roommate, Angela, are now on the suspects list, since Stephanie mentioned the argument last Friday. The fire marshal indicated the fire was suspicious. That begs the question, could someone have set the fire in order to cover up a killing spot?"

I shivered off the image.

"Inquiring minds want to know, as do the police."

"So now what?" I stacked a second pile of towels on the counter. The aroma of linen-scent Clorox filled the air. Mmmm, I loved the smell of clean.

"The fire was out by the time we got there," Tianna continued. "A few tendrils of smoke curled out of some charred floorboards of the storage closet on the side of the house. Still too hot to look for clues, but Meg says there should still be evidence they can collect if that's where the murder occurred."

I turned and faced her, my hand over my heart. "They don't think the actual murder happened inside my dog house?"

Tianna shook her head.

What a relief. I don't think any dog would be comfortable in a house that emits the aroma of murder. Dogs have ultra-sensitive noses, fifty times more sensitive than humans. Can you even imagine? The smell of not only death but fear? Which reminded me…"Did you happen to see the charred nail gun lying in the rubble?"

"Nope. I peaked in on the fire scene but there was nothing lying around."

"It could have been inside."

"One step ahead of you. I asked to use the restroom and did a quick look-see while I was inside."

"And?"

"Construction mess. Lots of tools. But no nail gun."

"So, a dead end?"

"No. I then asked Brittany if I could see her nail gun."

"Subtlety, thy name is Tianna Platt."

"I didn't say, 'Can I see the nail gun you used to kill Monique.'" Tianna shrugged her right shoulder. "I played like I was thinking of buying one and wanted to see how hers handled."

"And?"

Tianna leaned her hip against the counter and crossed her arms in front of her. "Brittany looked all around, but couldn't find it anywhere."

Hmmm…the plot thickens.

CHAPTER NINE

Here's what we need to do," I said, thinking out loud.

"What are you talking about?" Tianna asked.

I grabbed a broom and started sweeping up after this morning's dog washes. One had been a fluffy St. Bernard who shed five pounds of fur in the process. All of it currently on my floor. "I'm talking about determining if our suspects had alibis for the time of Monique's death." I poked the broom in her direction. "Move your feet, please."

She jumped over the ridge of swept fur and retreated to a clean corner. "What, you playing detective now?"

"I have taken it as a personal challenge to find out why the dead body was in my doghouse. So yeah, I'm playing detective now."

Tianna flashed me her one-raised-eyebrow, steely-eyed, sideways look. Translation: Have you lost your ever-lovin' mind? "You. A detective?" She snorted. "Good luck with that. But what's this 'we' business."

"I assumed you would want to be involved since you have a vested interest in clearing your name."

There was that look again. Tianna had a limited repertoire of "looks."

I swept the pile of fur into the dustpan and dumped it in the trash while trying to put the finishing touches on my plans before sharing my ideas with Tianna. If the plan sounded dangerous, illegal, or just this side of bat-guano crazy, then I'd get another look. Three "looks" from her in five minutes would be a personal best, but not a goal I desired to achieve.

The front door jangled. We had a customer. For a Monday, things had been pretty steady. Maybe the Bark-itecture event had been a good investment after all. I handed Tianna the broom and dustpan. "Finish up, will you please?" Flashing a crooked smile in her direction, I followed Mr. Belvedere through the saloon-style doors to help the customer.

"Welcome to Ruff Day Doggie Boutique. Feel free to browse. I'm happy to answer any questions."

The gaggle of shoppers had browsing down to a science, looking at and touching every single item in the shop. They then left without purchasing anything. "Cute shop," one said. "We'll be back."

I used to take it personally when shoppers didn't purchase anything. I mean, how could they *not* want to buy any of my lovely merchandise? But I'd quickly learned that was part of the retail business.

The saloon style doors swished and settled behind me. Tianna emerged, carrying two boxes of dog treats. We worked together to restock the display rack.

"Sorry, what's your plan?" she asked ever-so-casually.

Ah-ha. I had her hooked. "Any chance that Brittany has a dog?"

"I don't know."

"Maybe a niece or nephew with a dog? I'm thinking we could offer her and Emmaline Forrester—"

"Who is Emmaline Forrester?"

I gave her a quick rundown of my morning customer, currently my second POI. That's person of interest, for anyone not fluent in private investigator-speak. "We could lure them in with the promise of some sort of freebie. If we give them a specific time, we could both be here and casually ask what they were doing Saturday night."

"Subtlety is not my strong suit."

"You're right. Maybe I could casually ask, and you could casually observe to see if they're telling the truth. And, we could offer a coupon to your food truck and see if they'd eaten there and rave about your food. I still wondered about the significance of that food wrapper from your Jamaican Jubilee in the dead woman's hands."

"Yeah, me, too." Tianna shook her head.

"Okay, let's do it then." We high-fived.

Two phone calls later, both women agreed to meet us tomorrow morning. We high-fived again.

"Hey." Tianna broke down the cardboard boxes and set them by the door so that she could carry them to the recycle bin on her way home. "Did you tell the police about Emmaline Forrester?"

"I'm afraid putting a sixty-something woman up as a suspect in a brutal murder might sound a little crazy. If she doesn't have an alibi, I will."

"Promise?"

"Promise."

Tianna left. I began assembling small gift baskets to give as our freebie tomorrow. This would be interesting.

The door chimed. Hayden Burnside entered, looking all workday casual in his blue golf-shirt, Dockers and suede lace-up shoes. He and Tianna made a stunning couple.

I should also mention that he was not only the spark to my Bark-itecture flame, but he'd also designed my dog house. Who knew architects could wear hero capes?

"Hi, Hayden. You're back."

Mr. Belvedere hauled himself off his bed and greeted his friend.

Hayden rubbed the top of Mr. Belvedere's head. "Hi buddy." He looked up at me. "Yup, just rolled into town."

"Tianna left a few minutes ago."

"No worries. We're meeting for dinner tonight. I wanted to stop by and get your take on Bark-itecture."

"I'm sorry you couldn't be there."

"Me, too. But I couldn't miss the big biannual conference."

"Work before play. I get it. Did you discover some new trends in architecture?"

He nodded and smiled that charming smile that had hooked

Tianna. "So, tell me all about Bark-itecture."

"It was amazing, of course. And my dog house was the best, by far. At least in my opinion. Thank you for that awesome design and hooking me up with J.J. to build it. It sucks that it was off limits on account of, you know…" I couldn't bring myself to finish the sentence.

"Yeah, Tianna told me about that. God." He massaged the back of his neck, giving it a real good squeeze. "Monique was a head case, but she sure didn't deserve to go that way." He approached the counter in slow measured steps, rested his knuckles on the edge and leaned in. "You don't think, you know, that Tianna had, well, anything to do with it?"

Was he serious? My hands stopped their busy work, and I looked him right in the eyes. His troubled eyes. He was serious.

"I mean, is she the jealous type? Not that there was anything to be jealous about. I made it clear to Monique that this town wasn't big enough for the both of us, and she needed to move on." He pushed himself away from the counter. "Sorry. Geez. Forget I said anything. This whole thing has me pretty freaked out."

"Understandably."

He headed for the door, pausing, his hand resting on the handle. "I can't get Tianna's words out of my head. After meeting Monique, Tianna said to me, 'You get rid of that crazy slut, or I will."

And then there were three. Just don't tell Tianna she was now on the top of my POI list.

CHAPTER TEN

Tuesday. Ten a.m. Time for our first attempt at ever-so-sneakily extracting information out of suspects. I paced nervously around my shop. It took every ounce of willpower not to nibble on my nails. I mean, I'd never interrogated a potential witness before. And what in the world would I do if they didn't have an alibi? And then, oh, no. What if they knew I suspected them of murder and decided to kill me and Tianna to shut us up? Be still my racing heart!

Such are the downsides to an overactive imagination. You can scare the beejezus out of yourself pretty darn quickly.

The door jangled. Brittany entered, dressed ready for work in her blue waitress uniform, complete with hairbow, slightly askew (but who am I to judge?) "Hi," she said, rather breathlessly, as if she'd run here.

Before she could shut the door, Tianna raced in, once again dressed in t-shirt, jeans and Sketchers. She flashed me an "I'm sorry" smile and shoulder shrug.

I nodded and returned her apology with a "no worries" grin. "Good Morning, Brittany," I said as Mr. Belvedere gave his own greeting by standing next to the customer allowing (more like encouraging) them to pet him.

Brittany rubbed her hands along the top of his big head. "What a beautiful beast."

I had to agree.

She turned her attention to me. "I've never won anything before. I'm excited. And it came at the perfect time." She glanced

47

around the shop. "This is super cute!"

"Did you get a new dog?"

"Sort of. My roommate has one. I mean had one. I figure it's mine now since she was murdered."

I glanced at Tianna, who stood in the back corner by the clearance bin, arms crossed and eyes steely, staring at Brittany. Tianna took her role of casual observer seriously. So seriously that it bordered on guilty-until-proven-innocent. Not helpful. I coughed, getting her attention. *Pump the brakes* I motioned with my hands.

She slunk further into her corner and throttled back the intensity.

Brittany and I chatted about her new mutt. I piled more freebies into her basket, hoping that would garner customer loyalty. Brittany didn't seem at all upset with her new dog-mom responsibilities or the least bit distraught about the death of her roommate. That gave me the opening I needed.

"I heard about your roommate. Monique Mallicott, right?"

Brittany nodded.

"That whole thing was crazy. Any idea where she went Saturday night that would have ended in her death?"

"Nope. Last I saw of her was Friday when she showed up at work and made a scene."

"You didn't see her at all on Saturday?"

Brittany picked up her basket and headed for the door. "No, I had the weekend off. Angela, my other roommate, and I went to Raleigh. Alan Jackson played the PNC Arena. Great seats. Awesome time. Check out my Instagram. I posted tons of pictures. Thanks for this." With a flip of her hair and an over-the-shoulder smile, she left.

"She was at the concert," Tianna confirmed. She emerged from her corner and flashed me her phone. Brittany's Instagram page substantiated her claim of a Raleigh trip. Watertight alibi.

One down, two to go.

Emmaline Forrester arrived with Poppy in tow. The black Scottie oozed attitude and pranced right up to Mr. Belvedere.

He looked at the dog, then at me, then back at the dog. A

moment later Mr. Belvedere led Poppy to the toy bin. Poppy selected a squishy-squeezy octopus. *Squeak. Squeak. Squeak.*

Emmaline said, "Look at that. She loves it. I'll have to buy her one to take home."

I led her to the squeaky toy section, and then I followed behind her as she explored further.

She stopped at the Pup Tents, created specifically for beach dogs so they had a shady spot to rest while their owners soaked up the sun. "I'll take one of these, too." By the time she'd explored the last aisle she had added quite a few more things to her basket.

She was a happy, smiling customer.

I was a happy, smiling shop owner.

When it came time to check out, I accidently/on-purpose hit the reboot button on my cash register. I knew from too much experience it would take three minutes and twenty-nine seconds to fire back up. Time for *Operation: Where Were You Saturday Night.*

"Sorry for the delay," I said to Emmaline. "This happens too often. I need to upgrade my system."

She waved off my concerns. "I'm not in any hurry. And Poppy is fine. Seems she made a new friend."

Sure enough, the two dogs were cuddled up in Mr. Belvederes king-sized bed, taking turns squeaking the octopus. *Squeak. Squeak. Squeak.*

"So, did you have a good weekend?" I hope my nervousness didn't give away my snooping intentions.

"Not the best." She sighed. "I was in a car accident Saturday afternoon and spent the next twenty-four hours in the hospital."

"Oh, no. How awful," I said, reaching out and laying a comforting hand on her arm. I had read something about that in Monday's paper, but hadn't made the connection. The article hadn't mentioned any names, but said the hospital trip was out of an abundance of caution due to an unrelated underlying medical condition. None of my business, though. "I hope you're okay."

"A few minor bumps and bruises." She rubbed the back of her neck as if some stiffness remained. "Silly girl behind me was texting while driving. I stopped to let a dune fox cross the road.

She slammed right into the back of me."

Tianna tsk-tskd from her corner. She was anti text-and-drive. Big time. "I hope no one else was hurt," she said, uncrossing her arms and joining in the conversation.

"My SUV's a little worse for the wear, and the beach road is down one pine tree, but all's well that ends well." She rolled her shoulders, grimacing at the gentle movement. I don't imagine things ended as well for her as she professed. "How about you girls? Wild and crazy times?"

Tianna snorted. "If you call binging on cheese doodles and *The Marvelous Mrs. Maisel* a wild and crazy time, then yes, I did."

I laughed, a rather nervous, high-pitched laugh, because now the only POI without an alibi was my BFF.

CHAPTER ELEVEN

She's hiding something," Tianna said after Emmaline and Poppy left, over two-hundred dollars' worth of merchandise in hand.

"Like what?" I asked. "She's a seasoned citizen who stopped her car so she wouldn't run over a dune fox. She doesn't seem like the type who would kill a woman."

Tianna tapped her thumb against her lips, a sign she was deep in thought. "Even though she had an alibi, she could have hired a killer. Did you ever think of that?"

No, I hadn't. Goes to prove I do not have a criminal mind.

"I've got a few more questions for that woman." Tianna took off at a pretty good clip.

I leaned against the counter, my mind processing this concept. If Emmaline could hire a killer, then any of our suspects could have done that. Oh, Lordy. My POI list expanded to everyone on the planet. Not helpful.

How do police detectives do it? Solving cases like this? With so little evidence?

I shook my head and got busy refolding the stack of t-shirts, singing along to "Under the Boardwalk" as it played on my sound system. I'm convinced these t-shirts unfold themselves overnight, as this has become an onerous daily ritual. While folding and sorting I also took inventory. My biggest seller was a silhouette of a woman in a lounge chair, wine glass in hand and faithful canine companion with her. Slogan: Never Drink Alone. Only four shirts left. Time to order more.

The door jangled. I looked up. Hayden came over to me. But

this was not the metro-sexual Hayden who took great care with his appearance. This was a just-got-dragged-through-the-dung-heap-of-life Hayden, in a stained and rumpled t shirt, torn board shorts that didn't match, greasy hair poking out in many directions, and a day's growth of hair darkening his chin.

"Are you okay?" I asked, walking around the counter to greet him. I got close enough to see his eyes, dark and haunted-like. "What's wrong with you?"

"It's Tianna," he whispered.

"Tianna!" OMG, something happened to Tianna. But no, she'd left out of here less than fifteen minutes ago. Nothing horrific could have happened in that short period of time. Could it? No! Maybe! "What happened?" I practically screamed. "Tell me where she is."

"Calm down, okay?" Hayden sniffed, screwing up his face in the process. "Nothing's wrong. Not yet, anyway. It's just…" His voice cracked. "Have you noticed how she's hell-bent on finding Monique's killer?"

"We were both trying to figure things out. But yeah, she seemed a little more, how shall I say, motivated?"

"Do you know why?"

"Because the police suspect her."

"The police suspect her because she is the one who killed Monique."

"What?" I stepped back as if he'd just slapped me. Yeah, I know she was on my POI list, but I had never in my heart believed she had actually done it.

Hayden began pacing along the edge of the checkout counter. "I found a nail gun in her closet." He lifted his eyes ceilingward. His voice shook as he spoke the next words, "And it was covered in blood."

Oh. My. Gawd. That was the trifecta of a murder conviction.

Means: a nail gun. Found in her possession. And covered in blood. Monique's blood? Only a forensic scientist could tell for sure.

Opportunity: binging *Mrs. Maizel*? Seriously? Anyone who knows and loves Tianna will tell you she is all sci-fi, all the time, and I would testify to that in court if it came to that. Oh, how I hoped it wouldn't come to that.

Motive: jealousy, plain and simple. Tianna was a passionate and fiercely loyal woman. If someone moved in on her man, well, who knew what would happen? Except now we do know what would happen—murder.

I took a deep breath and expelled every bit of air from my lungs. "Oh. My Gawd," I said out loud, because it was on constant loop inside my head and needed to get out.

"My thoughts exactly." Hayden spun the rack of dog-themed cards, as if searching for the perfect humorous birthday greeting. It was obvious his mind was on something much more serious.

"Have you contacted the police?"

"I couldn't bring myself to do it. I thought maybe you could."

Me? Turn my BFF in for murder? Not bloody likely!

We argued back and forth a few times.

"Only one way to settle this," I said. "Rock, paper, scissors."

I counted, we displayed our hands. He showed paper, I showed rock. Paper covers rock. I lost. I always lose at rock paper scissors. I should have flipped a coin.

My fingers shook as I dialed the local non-emergency number and left a message for Officer Jurkowski, saying I had something urgent to talk to her about and could she come to Ruff Day to meet me.

Mr. Belvedere came and stood by me while we waited. I stroked his head mindlessly while I tried to come to grips with all this. I mean, my loving, caring, passionate Tianna! A cold-blooded killer!

The door chimed. In walked Officer Jurkowski. "What's up?"

I looked at Hayden. He looked beseechingly at me. I drew a deep breath and explained the whole thing.

"Where's the nail gun now?" Jurkowski asked. "I'm gonna need it for evidence."

"In a bag in my car," Hayden said.

"She hid the murder weapon in your car?"

"No. I put it there. I was afraid if I left it at her house then she'd get rid of the evidence."

Jurkowki rolled her eyes. She didn't think I saw it, but I did. I might have rolled mine, too. I mean, who in this age of police procedurals on television doesn't know you should never disturb potential evidence?

"I suppose it's got your prints on it?" Jurkowski said.

Hayden admitted it probably did. He hadn't thought of contaminating evidence in the emotions of finding a murder weapon in his girlfriend's possession.

"You'll need to come down to the station and get printed, so we can eliminate yours."

Hayden nodded. "I'll swing by this afternoon, if that's okay."

"Sure." Jurkowski rested her hands on her utility belt. "Any idea where the suspect is now?"

I cringed against that word. A suspect! Tianna!

As if on cue, the shop's door chimed and in rushed Tianna. "Well, that was a bust! We need—" Her sentence fell off as she took in the scene of Officer Jurkowski staring squint-eyed, Hayden looking like something the dog had dragged in, and me with tears streaming down my cheeks. Yes. Tears. I'm not sure when they'd started exactly, but there was no stopping them now.

"Tianna Platt, you have the right to remain silent."

I turned and rushed to the back of my shop. I couldn't bear to hear the rest of the Miranda rights.

But the sound I really wanted to avoid was that of handcuffs clicking around Tianna's wrists.

CHAPTER TWELVE

Even though I'd seen it with my own eyes, I still couldn't believe it. Tianna, arrested for murder. What does one do in a situation like this? Disavow the lifelong friendship? Or support her in her hour of need? Should you send a card courtesy of the jail? Does Hallmark even cover this kind of situation? *So sorry to hear of your recent incarceration.* Or maybe *Good things come to those who wait...in jail.*

I needed to hate Tianna, but I couldn't. My hate focused instead on Monique Mallicott. Why had she come to Bay Vista and ruined so many lives?

Now I felt guilty for hating a dead woman. A woman I had never met. And never would meet. Oh, gawd. What a mess.

I grabbed my phone and cyber-stalked Monique Mallicott. Maybe looking at her Instagram account would help me refocus my emotions.

Or not.

What I found knocked me on my butt. Literally. I had to take a seat on the bench by the dog washing station while my thumbs scrolled through screen after screen revealing some shocking truths.

Monique Mallicott had been a porn star. Not an overly successful porn star, but she'd made a few movies and had a respectable following on social media. I'll spare you the details of the cringe-worthy titles. And the plots are about as offensive as can be imagined.

Monique was trying to revive that career, teasing her

followers with news that she was "getting the band back together." In other words, her old on-screen co-star was back in the picture. A co-star named Sexy Sins. A co-star who had an uncanny resemblance to Hayden Burnside. I mean, really, freakily uncanny. Hayden must have an identical twin, although Tianna had never mentioned her boyfriend having a twin who starred in X-rated movies. But then again, that's not the kind of thing that comes up in polite conversation.

Eventually I got to Monique's Facebook page, which was a little tamer, but a lot more disturbing in that a photo posted from the night of her murder showed her at a party. Her escort? None other than Hayden Burnside. Of this I am certain. He wore the same golf shirt and dockers he'd worn into my store on Monday morning.

Mr. Belvedere brought his leash over to me and nudged it into my hand. Time for a potty break.

I did the murder math while we walked, trying to add Monique plus Hayden and coming up with two every time. That's the way math works. One plus one equals two. Never three. So, no room for another person. Tianna did not fit into the equation.

Had Hayden killed Monique and framed Tianna? I shook my head, trying to clear out that kind of crazy thinking. I mean, that bordered on maniacal. Hayden was not maniacal. I mean, he helped me design my whimsical dog house. Would a maniacal killer do that?

My feet, of their own volition, led us on a route past Hayden's beach townhome. I didn't realize it until we were standing next to his sleek silver Audi A3. It was parked, motor running, trunk open, at the curb in front of his house. I looked around. No sign of Hayden.

I glanced inside the trunk. It was caked in rust-colored dirt. It's not unusual to find bucketloads of sand in the back of a car, happens after a trip to the beach. But dirt like that?

But then it's not dirt, is it? It's dried blood. Lots and lots of dried blood.

Tucked in the corner sat a box of food-service wrappers. Not just any food service wrappers, but custom ordered green, gold, and black patterned ones. The kind branded to Tianna's food truck.

No such thing as coincidences, right?

Hayden had nail-gunned Monique to death.

A door slammed. The killer himself came out the front door of his townhome, two suitcases and one bulging duffle bag in tow. He glanced at me, tucked his head down and scurried toward his car.

"Going somewhere?" I asked. I sounded calm, although felt far from in inside.

He ignored my question.

"You killed Monique." The accusation was out of my mouth before I had time to ponder the consequences.

That surprised him. He set the suitcases down, ever so casual, and then hefted the duffle over his shoulder.

A blur of blue, and the damn thing whacked me upside the head. I fell backward, smacking my noggin against the Audi's bumper.

Mr. Belvedere lunged forward, teeth bared, at Hayden.

Hayden took off down the sidewalk.

Mr. Belvedere took off in pursuit.

Me? With the leash wrapped around my hand, I didn't have much choice. My arm snapped over my head, spun my body around, and then I was dragged along the sidewalks of Bay Vista.

I endured searing shoulder pain as my tendons fought valiantly to keep my arm attached to my body. I fought back waves of nausea as every bump in the sidewalk caught my hip bone, sending shooting pain all the way down through my toes. I suffered as each layer of skin was scrapped off my elbows, knees, chest, knuckles, and any other exposed body part.

Asphalt was worse, hotter, rougher, more painful. Bay Vista Drive. Five lanes of torture.

Tires screeched. Horns honked. People shouted. But we made it across without incident.

Once on the other side, my forehead smacked against the curb, my neck twisting unnaturally to absorb some of the impact.

A crunch echoed in my head. My nose. Oh, my nose! I was

this close to passing out. But I held on. I couldn't let Hayden get away.

The chase continued, the pace increasing with each of Mr. Belvedere's strides. My shoulder wouldn't be able to hold on much longer.

We hit the beach.

Scratchy sand found its way into my cuts and scrapes. Filled my mouth, ears, and eyes.

More people shouting.

Mr. Belvedere barking. *Woof! Woof! Woof!*

And then, as fast as it started, it stopped.

From my position flat on my back, I opened my eyes, looked up at the beautiful blue sky. Sweet bay air filled my lungs.

"You okay?" someone asked.

I honestly didn't have an answer to that.

Tilting my head—*ouch, ouch, ouch*—I found Mr. Belvedere standing two feet from me, all four paws pinning Hayden Burnside to the sand. "Um, yeah. You might want to call the police, though. That man under my dog is a cold-blooded murderer."

Speaking of blood, I was covered in it. Head to toe. My own blood.

And then I did the only thing a girl in my position could do. I passed out.

CHAPTER THIRTEEN

We sat on a blanket, Tianna and I, basking in the glow of the sun's lemon-tangerine rays. Gentle bay breezes blew across my face. A seagull squawked in the air above us. I dug my toes into the cool evening sand. Life was good.

"Time heals all wounds," Tianna said as way of a toast.

"I think you mean 'Wine heals all wounds.'"

"Yeah, that, too."

We clinked glasses.

I admired the rich, red color of the vintage Caymus Cabernet, the one hundred and fifty dollar a bottle stuff we'd always said we would spring for when we had something to celebrate. Tonight, we celebrated. Hayden was in jail. Tiana was out of jail. I was still alive. And Mr. Belvedere was a hero.

"You've got one hell of a story to tell your grandkids someday," she said.

I started to laugh, but that hurt. I offered a smile, but even that hurt. Everything still hurt and much was still bandaged, but I would be okay.

I lifted the glass to my lips. The wine tasted as good as it looked, with subtle notes of cocoa and dark ripe berries. I took another sip. And then another.

"So," Tianna said, settling back on her elbows. "Hayden killed Monique and tried to frame me. And you say he was a porn star! How could I have misjudged his character so much?" She shook her head.

I had been granted a meeting with Hayden—safety glass

between us—because frankly, he owed me some answers. Owed Tianna some answers, too, but she wasn't ready to face him yet.

"I think you judged his character just fine. He was a good person, and a faithful boyfriend. He told me the stud fees—his words not mine—from the movies paid for his degree in architecture. It was a means to an end. He had built a new life for himself, a successful and happy dream life with a girl he loved. Until Monique showed up and threatened to blackmail him and ruin all he had if he didn't come back for an encore. That was what they were doing, filming some test shots in J.J.'s woodworking shop when Hayden snapped and killed her."

"Yeah, but death by nail gun?"

I shrugged. *Ouch.* "It was handy. And he admitted to getting carried away, not realizing how much pent-up anger and embarrassment he'd bottled up inside."

"And he dumped the body in your dog house?"

"He wanted her to be found. Just not by you. He's sorry about that."

Tianna nodded, and then sipped her wine. "I guess we all have secrets."

"Yes, we do." I had enough wine in me to ask the question that had been burning on my lips for years. "Speaking of which, you ready to talk about your lost year yet?"

Tianna looked at me, and then dropped her hand and stared at her wine. "No big deal, really. I got in with a wild crowd, did some bad things, had a few run-ins with the police. Spent ten days in the pokey, an experience I never ever want to repeat, thank you very much. All history now."

"To history," I said, raising my glass before taking a few more sips of the tasty cabernet.

"No, forget the past. Let's toast to the future."

"I'll drink to that."

"You gonna be up for the Bark-itecture banquet tomorrow night?" she asked.

"Wouldn't miss it. I'm told to expect a bidding war on my whimsical doghouse. Seems the morbid provenance, having been designed by a murderer and harboring a dead body, has garnered a lot of interest."

"Good for you!"

"Good for the SPCA. It all goes to improve the lives of shelter dogs. That's what's really important." I thought about the day Mr. Belvedere had rescued me. Happiest day of my life. More people should experience that lifelong joy and companionship a shelter dog can offer.

"And good for Ruff Day Doggie Boutique, too, I imagine."

"Indeed!"

"I told you there was no such thing as bad publicity."

I nodded. "Business has quadrupled since Tuesday. People stopping in to hear the story of Mr. Belvedere catching a killer. They want their picture taken with the canine caped crusader. I'm thinking of redesigning my logo to reflect his superhero status."

"To Mr. Belvedere, and the continued success of Ruff Day," she said, in yet another toast.

"I'll drink to that!"

THE END

AT YOUR SERVICE

By Maria Hudgins

Trey and Kim are bichons who live with Jessica, a mystery writer who happens to be deaf. Trey is Jessica's incredibly intelligent and responsible service dog—Jessica's ears. Kim is a recent rescue with a horrid past. Trey and Jessica are determined to help Kim overcome her memories and learn to enjoy life. But someone is out to make all their lives miserable with threats, drones, and even fire. Jessica and her dogs enlist the aid of friends, police, and Trey's former trainer to find and trap the villain who is still after poor little Kim.

Maria Hudgins is a mystery writer and a former high school science teacher. She is the author of the Dotsy Lamb Travel Mysteries, the Lacy Glass Archaeology Mysteries and several published short stories. Her favorite things are traveling, reading, dogs, and cats. She lives in Hampton, Virginia with her cat, Lulu.

Website: www.mariahudgins.com

CHAPTER ONE

I am stone deaf and live alone in a large house, but I never worry about break-ins because Trey handles that sort of thing for me. He could raise the roof with his barking, and it wouldn't bother me because, as I said, I'm stone deaf. He could scare the bejeebers out of anyone who dared to enter without his approval, and, problem solved, pad happily up to me and explain what had happened. He can explain without words.

Trey is a sweet, three-year-old bichon, the small white fluffs of the dog world, and a highly trained service dog who takes his job seriously. I named him Trey because he's the third fluff I have owned and loved. Another dog, also a bichon, lives with us. I call her Kim because she reminds me of the young hero of Rudyard Kipling's book—small, white, and desperately poor. More on her later.

It started on an ordinary day when I was up in my third-floor observation deck. BTW, I am a mystery writer, and I publish under my real name of Jessica Chastain. Friends call me Jessie. Anyway, the floor started vibrating so I hurried down two flights of stairs, colliding with Trey, coming up. His little black button eyes danced with alarm. He reversed his path and led me to the front door and to Kim, standing there with blood all around her mouth. Was it Kim's own blood? I was afraid to stick my fingers in her mouth, given the excited state she was in, so I took a minute to sit, stroking her, and wait for her fury to subside. As I sat with her, I spotted a couple of light blue threads lying on the floor near the door. I grabbed them and twirled them between my fingers. Denim? Could have been from the fringe of my stylishly frayed jeans.

Kim settled down a bit and let me cuddle her. I ran my forefinger around inside her mouth, and she did not wince or complain, so the blood could not be Kim's. It must be the blood of whoever or whatever she had bitten. Squirrel or bird would be my first guesses, but Kim hadn't been outside since early morning. For one awful moment I thought it might have been a snake, but if so, where was it now?

In one of my most intelligent moves, I grabbed a white cotton facecloth and removed some of the blood from her teeth. I say intelligent because, even though I had no thought at the time of how it could be used for DNA analysis, I put the bloody cloth in a zip-lock bag and saved it.

CHAPTER TWO

I have not always been deaf. I lost my hearing in my late twenties because of an illness and a round of steroid treatments. Since I already had nearly three decades of constant talking behind me, I haven't been prone to develop the sort of throaty vocal tones one often hears in those who have never heard speech with their own ears. I usually have to tell people that I am deaf. Thank God, I've been born into a world with closed captioning and instant translations, even in phones. I have a landline that displays whatever my caller is saying, but my cell phone's closed caption feature works about as well as a third grader translating *Beowulf*. As long as I do all the talking, I can still use it. Face to face is no problem. I can read lips like a champ, and at home Trey often reminds visitors to face me. He touches whatever skin he can reach with his cold, wet nose. The doorbells, timers, smoke alarms, and fire alarms in my house are all rigged to flashing lights. And to Trey. If any of these signals go off, I soon feel Trey's nose on my arm.

I've had Trey since he was eleven months old. My best friend Nancy thought I needed a service dog—one that was specifically trained for the hearing impaired—and she just happened to know a guy who did such training. They introduced me to the sweet bichon puppy the trainer had purchased from a friend of a friend. The little guy was from what they call a puppy mill, but he was healthy, bright-eyed and beautifully trained. He settled into my home like Mr. Carson in *Downton Abbey*, efficiently directing events to make them easy for me. I soon found I was relying on Trey for things I can do for myself. Like answering the door.

Kim had a rougher start in life. It was about three months ago that Nancy came in and told me I simply had to see the dog she had found at the shelter. I wasn't inclined to go and see for myself. I already had a dog.

"It's a bichon—we think," she said.

"What do you mean, think?"

"Matted, dirty, skin and bones," she said, making a face. "You just have to see her. I'm taking her to the vet to see if he thinks she can survive. It's that bad."

Nancy is that sort of person. Can't stand to see anything in pain. I didn't want to go, but Nancy began to cry, and I can't stand to see a grown woman cry.

When I saw the poor little thing, I cried, too. "Why can't she walk?" I asked. "Is she too weak?"

The shelter attendant said, "It looks like she's been traveling for weeks. We don't know where she came from. We'll probably never know."

Long story short, the vet fixed her up, fed her for a couple of weeks, and Nancy and I took her to a groomer who cut off the matted hair and prettied her up. She was, in fact, a bichon, and a beautiful one at that. She was probably about four years old, and had given birth more than once.

When she met Trey, they soon formed a bond. The three of us settled into a happy routine of walks, games of fetch, and the two dogs playing in my fenced-in yard while I wrote stories in my office on the second floor. I named my new dog Kim, like in the Kipling story. I felt as if she made an effort to put her demons behind her and act like a playful, pampered, typical American dog. But she panicked whenever she was forced into a small space. The teeth bared when I put her into a carrier. She ran from strange men, and strained on her leash when we passed one on our walks.

CHAPTER THREE

Common sense told me Kim had not tangled with a bird or a squirrel or a snake. She was inside the house, and there were no such critters in my living quarters. She had bitten someone who had, somehow, come in without my permission. My best guess was a would-be thief had discovered an unlocked door. I told myself to be more careful. I can't expect Trey to remind me to lock up.

I had to report this biting event to the police, but I needed to do it in a way that would not reflect badly on Kim, who, after all, had been protecting our home. Police often forget that animals aren't necessarily the enemy. Dog bites man, they say, is not news, but quite often the dog is doing the right thing.

I called the police station using the closed captioning function on my landline. I gave my name and address and described the situation.

"My dog, Kim, has apparently bitten someone who was breaking into my house."

The screen on my landline scrolled: "You say apparently? Why apparently?"

"Because I didn't actually see the intruder. I heard a commotion." Not exactly. I felt it through the floorboards, but didn't want to explain that. "And I saw the blood on my dog's mouth."

The screen flashed and jumped to the policeman's response: "How did this person get into your house?"

"Through the front door, I think."

"Was the front door locked?"

"I think so."

"If it wasn't locked, it isn't exactly breaking in."

"I'm pretty sure it was locked."

"It might have been someone you know, just checking on you. After all, if the door wasn't locked, they might have been worried that something had happened to you. If so, you may be lucky you haven't been charged with harboring a dangerous animal."

"I'm sure it was an intruder. My dogs don't attack people I know."

This was not going well.

"Look. I forgot to tell you. I'm deaf and these are my service dogs." Slight inaccuracy here. One service dog and one pet. "My doorbell flashes a light in my office, and the light did not flash so nobody rang the doorbell. My dogs have let friends and service men in hundreds of times with no problem."

"Are there any other signs someone was deliberately breaking in?"

"Not really."

"Tell your service dogs to come to the station. We need to talk . . ." Here, the script broke off, I assume, because the officer realized his sarcasm was showing, and before he sank into something that could get him sued, he needed to close this out. "Yes, ma'am. I'll report this, but there isn't really anything we can do without more information."

CHAPTER FOUR

I climbed up to the third-floor observation deck I call my crow's nest. The only way to enter it is by the spiral staircase that leads up from the office where I do my writing. It's my escape from plot problems and back muscles strained by too much sitting at the computer. No more than five feet square, it has big windows on all four sides, a telescope, a pair of binoculars, and a well-thumbed copy of the *National Audubon Society Field Guide to North American Birds: Eastern Region*. From this spot, I can see the entrance to the Chesapeake Bay and, on a clear day, several miles out into the Atlantic. I can also scan parts of Virginia Beach, Norfolk, and the Hampton Roads Bridge Tunnel. I can survey my whole neighborhood, and, if I look across the eaves of my own house, I can check out parts of my front and back yards.

This was my favorite spot, even though it didn't have room for more furniture than a small upholstered cassock.

Sitting there, I pondered whether I should rethink my crow's nest, my second-floor office, my isolation from certain dangers that Kim had so vividly pointed out to me. How safe was I? Was I expecting too much of two little dogs? Who was that intruder and would he/she come back? Could I be wrong about the intruder? Could it have been simply a meter reader trying to tell me my meter was broken? My heart sank at the thought of giving up my crow's nest. It was my window on the real world. My source of great plots. My sanity. I couldn't think of giving up my crow's nest.

I gazed out the window again and spotted my dogs cavorting

in the front yard, their day back to normal. Time for a walk.

Trey doesn't need a leash, but Kim does. Like any well-trained service dog, Trey will walk beside me or in front of me or whatever is called for depending on the situation. He would never run away when he is working, but on this simple walk around the park, I hooked Trey up, so Kim wouldn't feel as if she alone was not trusted to behave.

Kim sniffed around the front gate and the ground along the fence as we moseyed down the sidewalk. In two or three spots, she stubbornly refused to move until she was satisfied. I knew that she would probably never be completely free of the traumas she had suffered in her past.

A well-toned man in baggy jeans jogged past us and sent Kim into a trembling fit.

I picked her up. "What's wrong, baby girl? Are you afraid of that man?" Her small, frame shivered against me.

Kim burrowed into the front of my unbuttoned cardigan as if being close to my body meant safety. Trey pulled on his leash, urging me forward. I put Kim down when she seemed to have recovered.

We progressed in a clockwise fashion around the park between my house and the community center. Had any of my neighbors seen someone walking into my yard that morning? Would they have noticed anything odd? Would they even remember? I couldn't possibly go around to each and every house that had a good view of my front yard. And how did I know he entered the front yard? He could have hopped the fence in the back yard and slipped around that way, where my yard backed onto a currently vacant home.

How about the Your Neighborhood email group? I thought about that, and I couldn't wait to get back to my computer.

Once inside the house, I let Trey and Kim off their leashes and logged onto the site. I typed my message: *My dog, Kim, attacked a person inside my house today, but they ran before I got there. Did any of you see anything unusual at my house, 375 Osprey Landing, this morning?*

In short order, I got several answers but nothing helpful.

That afternoon, Nancy dropped in for a chat. I loved the way Nancy made no attempt to disguise her sixty-seven years, but let her grey roam brazenly around her temples. She was an attractive woman who knew it and didn't care what people thought. She greeted the dog whose life she had saved with a scratch behind Kim's ears.

Kim wagged her tail.

Nancy settled in a chair at the kitchen table while I poured two glasses of Diet Pepsi with ice. I told Nancy about the excitement of that morning.

"Kim!" Nancy said, teasing. "Where were your manners?"

"This was not bad manners," I said. "Kim was ready to kill the—whoever it was."

"Man? Woman? Kid?"

"Don't know, but somehow I feel it was a man."

"Probably so."

I told Nancy about reporting the incident to the police and my futile attempt to find out if my neighbors saw anything.

Nancy took a sip of her Diet Pepsi and stared intently at Kim. "I have a strong feeling this has something to do with Kim's life before we found her. The vet was certain she's had at least one litter. Strange."

"Why?" I nodded toward her glass, silently asking if she wanted a refill.

Nancy shook her head. "Why? Well, because we know nothing of this little dog or why she was in that shelter in near-death condition. Why was she in that dump? A beautiful dog like this is usually a member of a doting family."

I said, "The shelter has the name of the kid who brought her in, but they talked to him, and he knew nothing more than the spot in the junkyard where he found her. It was in Chesapeake. South of here."

"What about that friend of yours, the one who trained Trey?"

"Allen?" Allen Lawson, a dog trainer, had received Trey

from a man who got him from . . . who? "Good idea. Allen may know something about where bichons come from."

"That, plus..." Nancy paused..."dogs are a lot like elephants, you know."

I laughed. "Not that I've ever noticed. Why do you say that?"

"They have really good memories." She looked down at Trey and Kim, both now lounging under the kitchen table. "And Kim has memories of her past. Is there any connection between bichons with no owners and this one found in a junkyard?"

We both knew it was a long shot, but I called Allen Lawson and explained why I wanted to know where, exactly, the dogs he trained came from. His students were all different breeds, but I figured he knew the market. He agreed to meet me at my house.

While I was on the phone, Nancy waved bye to me and blew a kiss at the dogs.

Allen drove to my house and, together, we went to work with his list of contacts. A big, athletic man in a lumberjack shirt, Allen barely missed being a "hunk" by virtue of being none too clean. His boots were dirty and his hair could stand a wash. Some of his contacts were clients, some were breeders, and some were suppliers of everything from veterinary dentistry to spikey toys. By mentioning that we were looking for a bichon, some of his contacts said, "I think I know someone you should talk to."

I pitched in and helped him by writing down everything anyone told Allen that seemed relevant. The owner who had sold Trey to Allen was easy to find. Allen remembered her. I had Trey's registration and knew that his official name was Royal Commander Pink Floyd, but we had to call the original owner to find the breeder. It was at the Holly Grove Kennels, some fifty miles south of me, where Trey had begun life. Allen told me it was a commercial dog breeding facility and known to be one of the worst.

The more Allen and I talked, the more we wanted to a) put the breeder out of business and b) get the owner, a man named Claude Raper, (oddly appropriate name!) arrested, convicted and sentenced to life in prison. Allen suggested the death penalty, but

I pointed out that would never fly in court. He told me some stories that made me want to cry.

The problem was that Raper and his so-called business had already been investigated by county officials who were keen to nab the guy under new Virginia laws that made what they found there a felony with serious penalties. Unfortunately, the investigators were unable to document any charges they thought they could make stick.

I felt like throwing up.

Allen moved his laptop aside, stood, and stretched. He agreed to put the word out that he would accept no more dogs without proof of ownership, but I said this wouldn't really help the situation. It might relieve Allen's own conscience, but would do nothing to keep these heartless jerks from continuing their cruel practices.

While Allen made a call to another client, I picked up Kim and cuddled her. I wished I could make all her memories happy ones. She snuggled more tightly into my lap and heaved a little sigh.

After Allen left, I was too keyed up to start cooking dinner. What else could I do? Like Allen, I had weapons in my arsenal; my blog, "A Study in Murder," I called it. In the last month or so, I had neglected my commitment to post one blog every week and, instead, I had called on some of my writer friends to fill in for me. But now I had a mission—to destroy Claude Raper, completely and irrevocably—and my blog could help get the word out to the world.

Some of the stories Allen had told me made my blood boil. I would skirt carefully around the problem of identifying him precisely in order to avoid being accused of libel. I would probably need to consult a lawyer at some point, but I sort of thought that a lawsuit with a rip-roaring court battle would be even better. I went online.

A Study in Murder: Vol. 10.4
September 20, 2020

Don't Shop! Adopt!

Friends, I have just found out that my dear little bichon, my best friend and right-hand dog, came from a puppy mill. The puppy mill from hell. We don't know any details, but I shudder to think of the conditions poor little Trey dealt with when he was too young to know that life could be better. I know I won't learn much more because this snake pit of a business doesn't keep records!

Of course, records would show none of their puppies had ever seen a doctor in their whole life. No vaccinations, no flea meds, nothing.

Many people today go to internet classified ads or independently managed websites that make the puppy look like he just stepped out of a suite at the Plaza. Don't be so gullible. If you are in doubt about a site, check out the help available from the Humane Society. Drop me a line or respond to this blog, and I will help you find out what you need.

Be an advocate for the little ones who can't speak for themselves. Check in to your state's laws and contact your own representatives. Many of them are on Facebook and Twitter.

If you want to know more about the scumbag breeder that operates this illegal business, contact me offline.

I re-read my blog several times before I posted it. I hoped I had given no information that would reveal Holly Grove Kennels as the object of my venom, but I knew readers would figure out the breeder was somewhere in the Mid-Atlantic area of the United States. I hoped the word would get back to Mr. Claude Raper in one way or another. Of course, he had no reason to connect the writer, Jessica Chastain, with my little Trey, so I hoped he would start suspecting anyone and everyone who asked a lot of questions. From my website, he would know I was deaf, and that I had adopted a service animal. He knew Alan Lawson was a trainer who sometimes bought puppies from local sellers. Both Alan and I reside in southeastern Virginia. Yes, he really might put two and two together. I almost hoped he would.

I checked my blog again later, and found I had several responses:

> Dear Jessica,
> My heart goes out to you and your little dog. I hope he's all right now. If you need a dog-sitter, I'm available and my rates are reasonable.

(That came from a fan who lives in California.)

> Dear Jessica,
> There is no punishment bad enough for people who abuse animals. They should all rot in hell. Or pay a fine.

> Dear Jessica,
> I have a five-year-old rottweiler named Arnold. I would never let him go near a puppy mill. You should keep your dogs away from those places.

I sat there, grinning over the nutty responses to my blog and wondering about the people who write these things. I've noticed these often come, not from my usual fans, but from the web-surfers called trolls—people who post mean things just to start an argument. Who *are* these people? Crazy to think some people have nothing better to do with their time than wreak havoc in the blog-o-sphere.

There was one final response:

> Dear Jessica,
> Thanks for the information. You better watch your back! I know where you live, now.

The comment came from "HGK." Holly Grove Kennels? Perhaps Mr. Claude Raper himself.

I shivered. Any man who would treat animals the way he did, would not stop at . . . what? What would he do to me?

I called both Allen and Nancy and asked for their advice. Nancy said I could move in with her for a while. I told her I didn't think things were that desperate yet. Allen gave me a tongue-lashing for being so stupid as to publish what he called "an engraved invitation to Claude Raper to come and get me."

"What would you suggest, Allen? We both know what he

does, who he is, and where he lives but the cops are no help, and the law is rigged in favor of the bad guys. I'm serious, Allen. What are *you* doing? I feel like I have to do something, even if it means taking some risks."

"Taking some risks is one thing. What you've done is not what I'd call a risk. It's asking for trouble!"

I returned to my computer and checked the Your Neighborhood site. I had six responses from would-be dog sitters, four from doggie day care businesses, and three from neighbors sending me pictures of their own dogs.

CHAPTER FIVE

The next morning, I leashed Kim and Trey for our walk and opened the front door. Thank goodness for small dogs and their noses. They froze in front of a brown paper bag on the welcome mat. A blivit. I had heard of these but never seen one. Never mind that the dictionary defines blivit as something annoying or pointless. The urban dictionary has another definition and, given the aroma, even I could detect this little present was of the urban dictionary sort. If not for the dogs, I would certainly have stepped on it.

Kim and Trey went rigid and began circling the smelly thing like kids playing ring-around-the-rosy. I slipped back into the house, grabbed a dust pan and consigned the stinky package to the city-owned garbage can.

I wracked my brain as we walked around the block. Who would have done this? It wasn't even close to Halloween, although the "trick" part of trick-or-treat seemed to have been eliminated since my own childhood. Nobody lets their kids do that sort of thing any more. I could think of no one who wished me ill except my newest adversary, Mr. Claude Raper. Was that the game we were playing? Home court bullying?

We reached the community center, the halfway point in our walk. My cell phone vibrated in my jeans pocket. Strange. I only take this phone with me in case of an emergency. I can make a call, such as to 9-1-1, but I can't hear what the other party is saying. I have a closed-caption app, but I find its printout makes little sense. I clicked on the call anyway and got a bunch of nonsense on a tiny screen. It was as if the caller was speaking a foreign language, or else he had the world's worst diction. I closed out the call and saved it for later.

Back home, I tried to return the call but couldn't. The number wasn't in my contact list, and I didn't recognize the area code. Something told me this was from a disposable mobile phone, sometimes called a "burner." Favorite devices of criminals and drug sellers. Given the fact that I had never before received a call from a burner phone, I felt sure the call had come from the "friend" who had left the present on my front porch.

Rather than give in to this harassment, I told myself to get a grip and get some work done.

Trey and Kim snuggled up on their pillows at the dining room windows and watched squirrels in the yard.

I hiked up to my crow's nest on the third floor, gazed out to the moody Atlantic Ocean, and studied the thin strip of beach that separated land from sea. Now late September, the surf-smoothed sand was speckled with walkers and dogs. They looked like ants from where I stood. The throngs of summer had mostly departed and left the beach to the locals. I wondered if my prankster had left his car at the beachfront and walked up this way, carrying his blivit. I had to smile at the thought that he could have stumbled and fallen on his paper bag.

———————

Bright and early the next morning, I took my coffee to the crow's nest and looked out the east window into the slanting rays of the morning sun. I glimpsed an odd-looking bird. It seemed to be heading my way. I grabbed my binoculars but didn't have time to properly adjust them before it came up to within a few feet of my window. What sort of stupid bird does that? I lowered the binoculars and saw that it was hovering. Hovering? It was a dull grey and about the size of—it was hard to tell at that distance—about the size of a crow. A crow?

A drone.

Quickly, it turned ninety degrees and took off to the north. I shifted my gaze to the north window. It sped off to the west, turned another ninety degrees, then another and back to the east, near the spot where I had first seen it.

Obviously, it was studying my house. I now had my very own spy, it seemed. A minute later the drone turned tail and left, but I lost track of it when it flew behind a patch of live oaks north of the community center. My heart pounded in my ears. This was getting serious. My home was being invaded, and I didn't even know what my invader looked like.

I called Allen on my landline and told him about the blivit and the drone. Allen had just gotten up and he lived some thirty minutes away, but he said he was coming right over.

I called the police and reported the same information to them. I had to remind them of my previous call about the intruder my dog had bitten. Given the sarcastic tone of the policeman on that call, I thought I might have been better off to omit the reminder, but they needed to realize today's events were not the first. This was a campaign of harassment.

Sergeant Hawkin was more receptive to my story than the first person I'd spoken to. It took no time at all for him to adjust to the slight pauses the closed captioning necessitates. I told him about the blivit and the drone. "I think I know who is doing this, sir. His name is Claude Raper, and he is the owner of the Holly Grove Kennels down near the North Carolina line."

"And how do you know this?"

"I suspect he's the one who responded to a blog I posted yesterday about puppy mills and their horrible practices. He told me to 'watch my back', and that he knew where I lived. Today I find a blivit at my front door, and there is a drone circling my house. I don't know why it's there, but I think drones can take pictures. This makes me nervous."

Sergeant Hawkin didn't answer for a minute. I figured he was writing this information down and possibly chuckling to himself. He promised to call me back after he checked out a few leads. I knew that really meant, *after I check out what you've told me and decide if you are a crackpot or not.*

Allen came in a few minutes later. He must have flown up

the highway. Trey was delighted to see his trainer again, circling all around him, tail wagging, until Allen reminded him he was a working dog and this sort of display was out of line.

Trey brought Kim up to him making sure his old trainer and his new friend were properly introduced.

We stood on the front porch while I showed Allen where the drone had come from and where it had disappeared to.

"It's no good trying to find the pilot now," Allen said, "He'll be long gone, but I'll drive over to that park behind the live oaks. There might be something there . . ." His voice trailed off as if he realized he had no idea what that something might be. "And another thing," he said. "You should stay with someone else for a while. I know these guys. Legitimate breeders are one thing, but these puppy mill guys are something else."

"You think he'll come after me?"

"He already has."

I called Nancy and told her what had been happening. She tried to persuade me to come and stay with her until this threat was over, but I wasn't ready yet to leave my home. It felt as if leaving would be letting him win. I wanted to show this jerk I don't scare that easily.

CHAPTER SIX

I was deep in the middle of a dream that promised to help me out of a plot hole my current story was trapped in. In this dream, my protagonist was running for her life from a burning warehouse, desperately searching for something she could use to . . . the smell of smoke was awfully keen.

Too keen. I rolled over, opened my eyes and drew in a breath.

Smoke! I sat bolt upright and sniffed again. No doubt about it. Something was on fire. I slid my legs off the side of the bed and felt something tug on my pajama bottoms.

Trey pulled frantically at my leg. Kim stood right beside him, bouncing, and, I'm sure, barking. I dashed downstairs and met a wall of smoke on the foyer at the bottom. I should have run out the front door at that point, but I couldn't help investigating. I had to know what was on fire.

Trey placed himself, stubbornly, in front of my legs, trying to keep me from going into the smoke, but I stepped over him. At the kitchen door, I met flames coming from the laundry room, from the dryer.

I grabbed for the extinguisher on the wall outside the laundry room door. I shielded my eyes with the corner of my pajama top and in my nervousness, fumbled for the pin, yanked it out, aimed the nozzle at the dryer, and squeezed the lever bringing on a snowstorm of oxygen-blocking foam.

In seconds the laundry room looked like a winter wonderland. But no signs of fire.

I turned and ran for the front door, grabbing my cell phone on the hall table as I dashed through. Trey and Kim were beside me.

We stood on the lawn. I called 9-1-1.

I told the emergency operator I was reading her words on my screen. That was an exaggeration. The screen was showing me gobbledygook. I was guessing at her words, but the important thing was that she should get my address down accurately.

She kept me on the line until the fire truck showed up, no more than three minutes later. Thank God for those lifesaving heroes. They ran through the house with their equipment, found that I had indeed put the fire out, but they still inspected the whole house and the vent opening on the outside.

One of the firemen led me around the side yard to my dryer vent to show me what had caused the problem. "We tell people to clean these vents often. Lint builds up in the vent and behind the dryer. It's one of the most common causes of house—" While he was talking, he was probing the vent with a rod. He paused, pulled on the hooked rod and out came, not the expected wad of lint, but a strip of burlap, so completely burned only a few spots of fabric remained to show what it had been. "What the—"

He pulled out the whole thing and sniffed. The blackened strip fell apart a couple of times, requiring him to probe deeper to get the rest of it. He called his co-workers over. "Gasoline. Someone has soaked this thing in gasoline and crammed it up the vent. This is arson. We gotta call the cops."

Fortunately, the smoke damage was confined to the kitchen and dining room. I would need to get new curtains for the dining room and foyer but a good cleaning with wood soap and wax would help a lot. I took all my linens to the laundromat and tossed out everything made of paper.

Needless to say, I had to move in with Nancy for a bit. I packed up my clothes, my laptop, and my dogs. Allen came over and helped me move a dog crate into Nancy's pantry beside the kitchen so Trey and Kim could have a spot to call home away from home. Nancy also had a dog, a nine-year-old basset hound named Eeyore. Until we actually reached the point of bringing the two new dogs into the domain of this older dog who had always been an only dog, I hadn't realized how lucky we were to have an actual trainer with us.

"We need to introduce the three of them outside," Allen said. His pockets were stuffed with dog treats. Allen had an aura about him of strength, peace, and security. No wonder dogs trusted him. Most important, Allen truly loved dogs. "Not in Eeyore's yard," he said. "It's part of his home. Let's go across the street."

We followed him to a little bus stop across the street and watched as Allen, the expert, led my two bouncy bichons and the aging, droopy, Eeyore through an elaborate meet-and-greet, with doggie treats.

Eventually, we all settled into Nancy's house with Kim and Trey taking a break in their crate and Eeyore asleep on his pillow. Allen joined Nancy and me in the kitchen, and pulled out a tall chair at Nancy's reclaimed barnwood bar. Hitching his jeans leg up at the knee and planting a boot on the chair's cross bar, he said, "I've talked to the police about your situation. They understand this is serious, and they've promised to keep an eye on this house and yours, Jessie. You'll probably see them driving past."

"Thanks," I said, and Nancy nodded.

"The state forensic lab has the burned burlap they pulled out of your dryer vent and a nice footprint they found on the ground under the vent. They've preserved it in plaster of Paris. We're going to make a case here. I hope."

"I hope so, too," I said. "I want that ass-hat to pay!"

"We all do, Jessie, but putting together enough hard evidence to make a court case isn't easy. And while we suspect Claude Raper, we can't prove it yet. We've got to tie him physically to your home—the drone, the fire, something."

"What about the email he posted on my blog?"

"Probably can't be traced to him. Maybe his computer, but not who actually posted it."

"The phone call?"

"Same thing."

Nancy had brewed coffee while we were talking, and was now filling three mugs. "What about the blivit?" She laughed and sloshed a bit of coffee onto the soapstone counter.

"Blivit's gone, right?" Allen said. "No evidence."

"What about the bloody washcloth?" I said. This came out of my mouth before I realized the possible connection. Might there be a connection between Claude Raper and Kim? Had my intruder been Raper himself? It was a stretch. My head began spinning with possibilities.

"Oh, right! I forgot about that." Allen slapped his own forehead. "You still have it?"

"Absolutely!"

"Take it to the police today," Allen said, half rising from his seat. "This needs to go to the forensic lab."

I had a moment of panic. Where had I put the cloth? It was in a sealed bag, but where had I put it?

"Nancy, watch the dogs. I have to go home and get that cloth. I think it's in the drawer where I keep my potholders. The cleaners are supposed to sanitize and throw away all the porous materials that can hold the smell of smoke. What if they've thrown it away?"

"Tomorrow," she said. "The cleaners are supposed to come, but they are always late."

———————

The next morning, I remembered I needed to go home and get the bloody cloth in the Ziploc bag. I dreaded walking into the smoky kitchen and seeing the laundry room that was now minus a dryer. It had been pulled out the day before, so the workers could repair and repaint the blackened wall. I had ordered a new dryer, and it was to be delivered soon.

The cleaners were already at my house when I drove up. An inspector from the fire department greeted me in the kitchen as if I were an intruder. I introduced myself.

"I'm just dropping by to pick up something I left in that drawer over there. Won't be a minute." As I approached the drawer beside the stove where I keep my potholders, I had a terrible thought: I had emptied that drawer the day before and taken its contents to the laundromat because everything porous reeked of smoke. Had I washed the bloody face cloth, too? My hand literally shook as I pulled the drawer open.

The drawer was empty.

I sank to the floor, furious at myself and feeling as if I had ruined my chances of making a court case that would nail the person who tangled with Kim at my front door. Had I taken the cloth out of the Ziploc bag before I tossed everything in the washer at the laundromat? I didn't recall pulling a soggy plastic bag out, and I surely wouldn't have thrown it in that big industrial-size dryer I'd used. It would have melted. I cast my mind back to yesterday's actions in the kitchen. I saw myself cramming everything, dish towels, potholders, padded gloves, into the laundry bag and . . . aha! My mind's eye flashed on a hazy memory. As I was pulling everything out, I had hesitated and picked up the Ziploc bag, held it briefly, and realized it shouldn't be laundered with the rest. Rather than finding a safe place to keep it, I had slipped it in the knife drawer because nothing in there needed to be cleaned.

I scrambled to my feet and turned to the counter, opened the knife drawer and there it was. I could have kissed it. The blood on the cloth, I noticed, had turned a dark brown, but that wouldn't keep it from responding to a DNA analysis. I had written enough mysteries that hinged on DNA to know that.

I hurried with the bag to the police station.

Our local police station seemed to have only two officers dealing with the general public: the good cop and the bad cop. The sarcastic one who had answered my first call, and the nice one named Sergeant Hawkin who had followed up on my report of the blivit and the drone. This time I got the sarcastic one.

I pulled the Ziploc bag from my purse and laid it on the counter. I explained that the blood on this cloth came from my dog's mouth after she had bitten the intruder I felt sure was the cause of all my problems, including the fire.

"Useless," he said, practically sneering at the plastic bag. "We have a protocol we call chain of custody. If you can't certify who has had evidence in their possession from the time it is found until it is registered in court, it is useless."

"I know that. I write mysteries. I know all about your rules of evidence."

He lowered his eyebrows and leaned toward me as if he had been waiting his whole career to cream a writer with his knowledge of police procedure. "Lady, if I could tell you all the stupid mistakes I've read in those books that make it onto Amazon—"

I cut him off. It had been a long time since anyone had called me a lady in that tone of voice. "I take it that you don't intend to get this tested?"

"We don't use the taxpayers' money to cater to the whims of amateur detectives."

"Thank you," I said and walked out with my bag.

CHAPTER SEVEN

It was time to draw on my associations in the mystery writer community. Hundreds of writers, every day, paused their hands over their keyboards to ask a forensic question that, if handled wrong, would send readers across the country into fits, and books flying against walls. But mystery writers help each other with their questions, and we have a few forensic experts who volunteer their services. I called upon one of my favorites and soon had the name and address of a local private lab that would do DNA analysis, often faster than the state labs could get it done. And their work was absolutely reliable. I messaged them and arranged to bring my bloody cloth to them the next day. This was not going to be cheap, they warned me, but I didn't care.

We settled in Nancy's house for the evening. Her kitchen was cozy and inviting, with a sort of country feel. I volunteered to do my special Chicken à la Stanley, which I like to serve with rice, asparagus, and salad.

While I cooked, the three dogs dozed in their own special spots—Eeyore on his pillow in the corner, Trey and Kim on blankets in the crate Allen had settled in the pantry and within sight of the kitchen. Nancy and I shared a bottle of Merlot she had been saving for a special occasion, and I was pleased that she considered our visit a special occasion. She told me some funny stories about Eeyore as a puppy, tripping over his own ears, and snooping into a hollow log filled with bees. My laugh woke up the snoozing hound. He lifted his head and bayed. Trey and Kim woke up and added their own little yips and squeaks to what must have sounded like a canine chorus.

"I need to go back to my house tomorrow," I said, spooning Chicken à la Stanley onto a mound of rice. "I want to find out how long the cleaners need to work there. They're repainting the laundry room and repairing the wall where the dryer used to sit. But I have new dining room curtains being delivered, and I need to get more clothes."

"How about I go with you? I'd like to see what you're dealing with," Nancy said.

———————

The next morning, I took the bloody cloth to the lab. My writer friend, the forensic expert, had already called them and greased my path for an easy admission. It pays to have friends. They advised me that the sample was undoubtedly contaminated with DNA from at least three sources—my dog, the person bitten, and me—but they could eliminate my own genetics by where on the cloth it was found. And that would leave only human and canine DNA to separate. The technician in the white lab coat looked too young to be out of school yet, but the older I get, the more everyone looks too young to be out of school. She promised me that differentiating between the human and dog DNA would be no problem.

"And I'll be able to tell you what breed of dog it is and, probably, what kind of kibble it eats."

———————

Nancy and the dogs were waiting for me at Nancy's house. We drove from there back to my house. I understood that my new clothes dryer was to be installed that day, and that painters would be working on the dining room walls.

I closed the gate behind us, so the dogs could play while Nancy and I went in. Trey and Kim raced to the plastic bucket in the corner of the yard where they keep some of their toys but Eeyore stayed close to us. His wrinkled old legs struggled to make it up the steps. I fumbled with the keys while Nancy waited.

"Eeyore? What do you find so interesting?" Nancy's dog was

sniffing, nose to the porch floor.

"Do you suppose he can still smell the blivit? That's where it was, but that was days ago," I said.

"Of course he can still smell it. Basset hounds' noses are as good as bloodhounds'. Eeyore may be old but his nose is still Olympic class."

Eeyore continued sniffing the porch floor, his rib cage pulsing rapidly, turning round and round as if he was looking for something that ought to be there. I opened the front door and stepped inside, but Nancy held back. "Jessie, I think he's onto something. I'm trying to pull him into the house but he's pulling against me."

"But there's nothing here to find. I can see that for myself. Everything is as usual," I said.

"Let's humor him. He rarely gets to call the shots."

I dropped my purse in the foyer and followed them.

Eeyore sniffed the post at the head of the steps, then did the same for the next few balusters. He couldn't quite make it down the steep steps while sniffing, so Nancy helped him with two hands around his mid-section.

"What's he doing now?" I asked.

"Lord only knows."

At the base of the steps, Eeyore weaved back and forth and back and forth, on both sides of the flagstone path between the front gate and the porch, then headed for the south side yard in the opposite direction from where Kim and Trey were. They were playing on the north side of the house, but Eeyore obviously wasn't tracking them. He stopped several times, sniffing, turning, back-tracking, but never pausing in his self-appointed task. I was fascinated. What was he smelling?

Nancy held his leash but did not force him to go any particular direction. Eeyore was in charge. He sniffed his way around to the laundry room, headed for the now-blackened vent and stepped back, baying sadly, and I supposed it was the lingering smell of smoke and gasoline that he didn't like. He weaved back and forth around that area, still sniffing.

"There's something here," Nancy said. "He's looking for

something that's . . . oh, I don't know."

He continued his zig-zag pursuit of something we could never smell. He seemed to have come to a dead end when he moseyed toward the fence that marked the boundary of my property. My heart sank a little, and I realized I had let myself hope he would head straight for the dryer vent and point to something important. Maybe a gas cap or a knife with burlap fibers still attached. I knew the investigators had already found a suspicious footprint.

Eeyore stopped before he reached the fence and sniffed the ground.

"I think he's found something," Nancy said, tightening her grip on the dog's leash. "Careful, boy, just sniff. Don't eat."

Approaching the spot where Eeyore stood, I spied a small, white something in the grass. I bent over it for a closer look. "A cigarette butt."

"You don't smoke," Nancy said. "Who dropped this?"

"The fire investigators don't either. I talked to one who was here. He told me their department had been so badly affected by the effects of careless smoking they had all quit, and the department now had a strict rule: no smoking on the job." I started to pick up the cigarette butt, then remembered about the chain of custody. I had learned that lesson with the bloody washcloth. I could pick it up without touching it, but who's to say a clever lawyer in court couldn't get this thrown out by saying it was contaminated with my DNA? We'd had no rain since the fire. If this butt had been here more than a week, it would have been rained on. Who, other than firemen and workmen had crossed this side yard in the past few days? I couldn't eliminate the possibility that one of the workmen, perhaps the ones who had worked on the laundry room wall, had left this here. I decided to collect this anyway. The painters were supposed to come today. Were they in the house now? They could act as witness.

"Hold Eeyore," I told Nancy. I looked toward the street. Thank goodness a panel van with Beach Interiors" on its side was parked at the sidewalk.

I rushed inside my home. In the dining room, I tapped one of the two painters on his shoulder. "Take a break. I've got a little job for you." He sleeved his brush in plastic and followed me out. These workers were here for the first time, so I knew the cigarette butt couldn't be blamed on them. "I want you to be my witness. I'm going to pick up a cigarette butt and put it in a bag and I am not going to touch it. If it ever comes up again, I want you to back me up."

"Is this going to get me in trouble?" He took a small step backward.

"Absolutely not. It probably means nothing anyway."

With Nancy, the painter, and Eeyore as my witnesses, I used my phone to take a picture of the cigarette butt in place, then opened the small bag and drew the butt in while keeping my fingers on the outside of the bag. I zipped it closed. Back in the house, I grabbed a piece of note paper and wrote the date, time, and place, then had Nancy and the painter sign as witnesses. I stuck the paper and the bag in a drawer in my office upstairs, walked back down to Nancy and the wide-eyed painter, both of whom, I imagined, wanted to laugh but didn't. As an afterthought, I set a penny at the spot where the cigarette butt had lain and took another picture of the coin as it lay in the grass.

"Can't be too careful," I said. "You never know what will be important."

That evening, I called Allen and told him about my discovery. On my cell phone screen, I saw only a weird bunch of nonsense. Allen was laughing at me.

"Way to go, Sherlock," I read when the text cleared up. "I'm driving to the Holly Grove Kennels tomorrow. Do you want to go with me?"

The thought of visiting a puppy mill set my stomach to churning. I wondered if I could handle it. What would I say? "Why are you going?"

"My excuse for going is to talk to Raper about a standard poodle I'm working with. My real reason is to see if I can find anything the state inspectors missed. We need to nail this guy."

I nodded. If I went with him, I would have to carefully plan what I would say. I needed more time. I told Allen I couldn't go, but I wanted him to call me as soon as he got back.

CHAPTER EIGHT

When the first rays of morning sun slanted through the bedroom window, Kim came to the side of my bed, obviously in distress. I was sleeping in Nancy's guest bedroom on the first floor. Trey and Kim's crate sat in the pantry between this room and the kitchen. We had not been keeping the dogs' crate locked because there was no need to do so. "What's the matter, baby? Where is Trey?"

She danced around in circles, darted toward the door and back to my bed, then bounced, yipping and pawing at my bed covers. I flew out and around to the pantry and saw the crate—open and empty. "Where's Trey?" I said.

I looked all over the downstairs and didn't find him. Maybe he's upstairs? Nope. I retraced my steps, looking for possible escape hatches. No windows were open. All doors were closed.

"Nancy," I called into her bedroom. "I need your help, please. Trey is missing."

While she was getting her head together, I grabbed my slippers and stepped outside. Nancy's yard was not fenced in as mine was. Her front yard was open to the street. No sign of Trey.

Now I began to panic, but I told myself that panic creates more problems. Could he have found his way into the basement? Chasing a mouse or something? Nancy's house had no basement. Garage? That must be it. He got into the garage through the kitchen and the door closed behind him. Not likely, but possible.

What about the side door between the yard and the kitchen? I decided to try it first, even though it was almost certainly locked. I unlocked it from the inside then stepped out. As I reached out toward the knob, I saw the scratches.

Fresh scratches along the gap between the door and the frame, in line with the center of the knob. It was the simple type that could be locked and unlocked from the inside with the twist of a button and unlocked from the outside with a key.

Or with a tool. The lock had obviously been jimmied.

I ran back in and told Nancy.

She set to work calling neighbors, reporting the break-in, and checking the house to see what was missing. Meanwhile I scanned every room again. Kim followed, virtually glued to my leg. Nothing was missing except my little Trey. The police had been told to keep an eye on both my house and Nancy's. I didn't know how often they would check, but if they had been patrolling the neighborhood, they could have seen something.

I called Allen and reported the dognapping of his former trainee, Trey. He was already in his van, preparing to leave for his trip to the Holly Grove Kennels. "Stay put," Allen told me. "I'll be right over."

Thirty minutes later, Allen, Nancy, and I commiserated over coffee at the kitchen bar.

"Who would steal a three-year-old bichon?" I asked. "Bichons are a really popular breed, but break into someone's house and steal one? I don't think that's likely. Someone took a huge risk."

"But a service dog like Trey?" Allen said. "A dog that has been trained like Trey? Training alone costs maybe twenty-five thousand dollars and a trained dog can cost—" He blew out his breath. "I've seen them go for up to fifty thou."

"That's motive enough for some people, but would Trey be useful for anyone other than a hearing-impaired person?" Nancy asked.

"Most of his training was related to paying attention and following orders. It would be fairly easy to train him to help in other ways, say, for medical emergencies or mobility issues."

"This still isn't adding up," I said.

"We are ignoring the obvious." Nancy slapped her hands on

the countertop. "The reason you are here, Jessie, is because someone tried to burn your house down and all signs point to Mr. Claude Raper who, incidentally, owns the place where Trey was born. State inspectors are on his back. We know this guy is pissed off at Jessie for the stuff she put on her website. She's threatening his business. He's threatened. I don't think this is a mystery at all."

"But why steal Trey?" I said.

Both Allen and Nancy sort of froze, as if they hadn't considered the possibility Trey's value as a pure-bred bichon and a service animal weren't reasons for the dog-napping.

"Claude Raper wants his dog back. Maybe he just wants to cause Jessie more trouble," Allen said, musing.

"He has no use for a male. A few sperm donors are all he'd need. It's females he needs."

"You'd think he'd want to steal Kim. He'd be dumb to steal Trey. Plus, I've had Trey microchipped—with my name and address and everything."

"By the way," Allen said, "Is Kim microchipped?"

"Yes." I said.

Allen twisted on his bar stool and shifted his weight. He squinted through the window to Nancy's backyard. "I won't go so far as to say all bichons look alike, but they do have a strong family resemblance."

I grinned and nodded.

I know we all three wanted to laugh, but this was too serious, so we all just nodded. The dog-napper may have grabbed the wrong dog.

Time for me to meet this dog-napping scumbag. I was going to Holly Grove Puppy Mill.

———

We hit the road before ten the next morning in Allen's Chrysler minivan with the service dog logo on the side. I knew Allen wasn't married, but I didn't know if he had been previously married, if he had kids, or what. The fact that some of the back seats in his minivan had been flattened and others completely removed told me he didn't often have passengers. The whole back half of the interior was empty but for some blankets and a couple of dog carriers in varying sizes. The inside smelled of dog.

The whole reason for Allen's trip had changed. He originally meant to demand to see records Raper had told the earlier inspectors were at his accountant's. Now, all he wanted was Trey back.

Motoring south, Allen and I had to adjust to the main problem I always have in cars: the difficulty of lip-reading when everyone is facing forward. Riding shotgun, I had to keep poking Allen on the arm to remind him, and he had to deal with keeping his eyes on the road while turning his face toward me.

Allen's GPS led us down country roads which led to narrow, unpaved roads, and finally to a muddy, cratered lane that was so bumpy I was afraid the van would turn over or get stuck. On both sides, acres of golden-brown corn stalks, long past harvest, rattled in the warm fall wind. I wondered aloud if we were on the wrong path because there were no signs to the Holly Grove Kennels.

"Signs?" Allen said. "He doesn't want visitors. Why would he post signs?"

That thought gave me chills. It seemed as if a cold, grey blanket had descended on the land. What would I do when I finally saw the female dogs in kennels? Would some have puppies with them? Would they be clean? Would they have clean water? Would they all be barking at the same time? I wasn't prepared for what I might see.

The Holly Grove Kennels were at the dead end of the lane. I was surprised to see a brick rancher to the left of the cinderblock building I assumed housed the dogs. I hadn't considered the fact that the owner had to have some place to live unless he lived offsite. Several derelict vehicles in the yard took the place of any grass that may have once grown there, and a satellite dish was strapped to the chimney. One lonely little tree, maybe an elm, struggled to survive in the space that had been taken over by rusting iron. But surrounding the whole property, a sturdy, eight-foot fence dared anyone who came this far to come any farther.

Our vehicle sat in front of an iron gate closed with a steel cable and padlock.

"Now what?" I looked at Allen who was studying the forbidding sight through the windshield.

"You stay here," he said. He stepped out, walked forward to the gate and examined the cable that held it closed. He stepped to both sides of the gate looking for, I thought, a speaker box. He stepped back, looked up and down the long stretch of fencing, then came back to the van. "No way to let him know we're here. I could yell, but I don't think it would do any good. I'll call him." Allen grabbed his phone off the van's center console and scrolled down his contacts list. He hit the dial button and waited. And waited. After what must have been a dozen rings, he stepped away from the van and yelled something toward the cinderblock building. That didn't work either. Allen turned toward me and shrugged, hands out, as if to say, *now what?* "If that bastard has left—"

"Should I go with you?" I said, my pulse quickening.

"You stay here," he told me firmly, leaving no room for discussion. I figured it was for one of two reasons. Either Allen was protecting me from a meeting that might turn ugly, or he knows how upset I am and he worries that I might lose it and attack the man. I've never physically assaulted anyone in my life, but then I've never had a dog kidnapped. This was one of those situations for which there are no rules. Allen is a soft-spoken guy whose large frame makes its own statement. As an animal trainer, he would not have the patience to work with puppies if he lost his temper easily. Now, I, on the other hand, work with a laptop and what's in my own head. Why would I ever lose my temper? I can quit whenever I want to.

I looked at the bleak building beyond the gate, the muddy ground around it, the stack of old wire cages on one side, lightbulbs hanging from bare cords draped over clothes lines strewn with dingy towels, and thought about Trey starting his life here. Of course, he wouldn't have had anything better to compare this to, but I'll bet Trey thought Allen's place was heaven when he found himself there.

Allen checked his phone again and, I assume, hit redial, waited a bit, pressed another button, and turned back to the van. He had a resigned look on his face. Then, I spotted a man coming around the corner of the cinderblock building. I tapped on the windshield and pointed.

The man, wearing dirty old overalls and waders, plodded up to the gate and talked to Allen, but of course I couldn't hear any of the conversation and Allen's back was toward me, but I could see the man's face, and he did not look happy. They talked for several minutes.

The man pulled a ring of keys from his pocket and opened the gate. Allen stepped forward, turned toward me, then back to the man. He stood in the opening but did not go all the way in. I assumed Allen and the man I was pretty sure was Claude Raper were discussing whether Allen could drive the van inside the gate. I would have given anything to know what they were saying to each other.

Allen's left hand was balled into a fist. His right was clamped tightly on his phone. His shoulders looked tense.

The man's face was clean-shaven and weathered. Bushy eyebrows, knitted, eyes narrowed, and lips that revealed crooked, yellow teeth as he spoke.

I didn't know at that moment if I hoped Allen would come back to the van and drive us inside, or come back to the van and make a U-turn in the mud.

I looked past the argument taking place at the open gate and saw a little ball of white fluff running hell-bent for leather straight toward us. It ran like a flash between the man's legs, and leaped into Allen's arms. It happened so fast, I didn't have time to notice the man's reaction. Allen turned and ran to the van, cradling his precious bundle. He handed Trey to me and threw the van in reverse gear, spinning his tires in his haste to get out of there.

Trey licked me all over my face. Allen's van careened and bounced through the obstacle course of potholes and boulders, speeding back to the nearest paved road. He slowed down and turned to me. "You'd better put him in a carrier in the back. On this road, he could be thrown against the windshield."

I realized Allen was right, but I couldn't stand to let Trey go. I wanted to hold him forever. So, I scrambled over the center console with my little helper and crawled on my knees to one of the carriers, put Trey in it, then sat cross-legged beside it. I intended to ride all the way home this way. "What happened back there?," I said. "Was that Claude Raper? Did he admit he had stolen Trey?"

Allen turned his head around far enough for me to see his mouth. I realized I had forced him into a dangerous position, driving while turning his head. "Yes, that was Raper. He admitted nothing. I told him I knew he had your dog, but he said I was crazy. He wanted to know who I had in the van. I told him it was none of his business. He said I could be arrested for trespassing. I said I wasn't trespassing unless I came all the way through the gate."

"Sounds like a real intelligent conversation," I said, sticking my finger through the zippered opening of the carrier so I could touch Trey's fur. This wasn't working. I asked Allen to pull over for a minute.

He stopped, and I slid Trey's carrier to the gap between the front seats and behind the center console, then crawled over and back into the shotgun seat. I could see my dog's head through the mesh window of the carrier. He was watching me. I reached back and rested my left hand close enough for him to smell me. Now Allen and I could talk more comfortably.

"Oh. Did I yell anything real loud while I was at the gate?" Allen asked.

I thought about it. "No. Not while you were at the gate, but while you were standing outside the gate trying to call him, it looked like you were yelling something."

"That was it!" Allen smacked the steering wheel with his hand. "I did yell. That must have been when Trey heard me. I don't know where Raper was keeping him, but he must have had him somewhere Trey was able to escape from. I'd love to know where he was and how he managed to get free."

"I would, too, but I don't want to go back and ask." I looked back at Trey, now lying somewhat more calmly in the little dog carrier. "This is the smartest dog I've ever seen," I said. "I wonder how he got loose."

"Hopefully, we will meet Claude Raper again in court. You can ask him then."

CHAPTER NINE

I had tears in my eyes watching the reunion of Kim and Trey. They chased each other around Nancy's yard until they both flopped, exhausted, into the grass. Eeyore watched dolefully from a distance.

Allen and I had stopped off at Subway and bought three subs because we were hungry, and I knew Nancy wouldn't have prepared any lunch. We sat at the breakfast bar in Nancy's kitchen and talked. As she poured iced tea for all three of us, she asked me what I planned to do next. "You can't let this drop, just because you've got your dog back."

"Don't worry. My brain is spinning with ideas about what to do next. I'm not going to stop until I put that man out of business."

"I think you can do a lot more than that," Allen said. "Jail time. The man tried to burn down your house with you in it."

"Dognapping," Nancy said.

"Stalking," I added. "The drone, you know."

"Home invasion," Nancy said. "When you get the lab results from that washcloth, assuming it has Claude Raper's DNA on it, you have proof he came into your house without your permission."

"The blivit?" I added, still not able to mention the blivit without laughing.

"I don't know," Allen said. "Vandalism? Reckless endangerment?"

"That may be going too far. Maybe I can add that to the

103

stalking charge. More evidence."

"I reported my break-in to the police this morning," Nancy said. "I took pictures of my scratched-up kitchen door to them."

"We, all three of us, have to write down all this stuff while it's fresh in our minds: dates, times, and with all the details—it may be months before this actually goes to court," Allen said.

"The fire marshal is drawing up arson charges for me," I said. "He's helping me with the insurance claim, and he knows how to handle the legal requirements."

Lunch now over, it was time for me and my dogs to pack up and move back to our own house. With Allen already there, he could help me with the crate. I hugged Nancy and told her I owed her a big one. Eeyore didn't even wake up to tell us goodbye.

I settled into my house, hoping the smell of smoke had been permanently banished from the walls and floors. New drapes in the dining room and new curtains in the kitchen helped cheer me up. I'd been wanting new drapes anyway.

Back in my writing room, I logged on to catch up with mail on my blog. Time for an update. I wanted my readers to know the latest, but I couldn't use Claude Raper's name because he had not yet been charged with anything, and I certainly didn't want to jeopardize my case against him.

What should I tell them? I reviewed the last couple of weeks in my mind's eye, as if it was a movie. It hit me like a cannon ball. This had been about Kim, not Trey, from the beginning! It started with Kim biting the intruder—Claude Raper. Why? Because she had once been Raper's captive bitch, and she hated him more than anyone on earth. Because she had saved her own life by running away, almost died, and here he was again. He would take her back to misery. Everything else had flowed from that event and from my comments on my blog.

A Study in Murder: Vol. 10.5
Sept 25, 2020
Help! Dognapper!
You know how much I depend on my service dog, Trey, but

I never thought Trey would have to depend on me to save his young life. This is actually a continuation of my earlier post about badly-run puppy mills and the conditions that I now know led my adoptee, Kim, to run away from the unbearable conditions in the one where she was confined. I couldn't let the situation go unaddressed and I suppose I angered the kennel owner, because my life has been a living hell for the past few weeks. Pending charges keep me from going into details, but without naming names, let me just say that Trey was kidnapped by mistake.

The thief obviously wanted Kim when he broke into my friend's house. (I've been living with this friend while my own house is repaired. More on that later. Charges pending, you know.) Anyway, the thief who broke in in the middle of the night picked up the wrong dog from the crate they both were staying in. Bichons look remarkably similar to one another.

I made a police report, of course, but they had no probable cause to travel outside the city to the kennel where I was pretty sure Trey could be found. A friend and I had to do this ourselves. If Trey had been a person, all stops would have been pulled, and it would have been all over the news, but—okay, I understand—everyone doesn't feel as strongly as I do about the treatment of animals.

But Trey actually saved himself. From wherever he was being held, he heard us, broke free and scampered to freedom through the legs of the criminal I'm determined will pay. Let's hear it for dogs! They are smarter than we are.

I put in another plug for adopting, rather than purchasing, dogs. Scrolling down the blogsite, I found more cheery messages from Claude Raper. His previous signature was HGK, but now he had a new display name: Pupdaddy. How cute. The mental image gave me the creeps. He had been busy. A dozen hate-filled messages sullied my beautiful blogspace and left no doubt that I was in big trouble. One of them read:

I know a little girl who needs to come home. If the person who is holding her would wise up, she could save herself a lot of pain. She thinks she can hide by moving to her friend's house? Not gonna work.

At this point, I was beyond caring about threats.

With two clicks, I saved a copy of the message in a folder named "Holly Grove Kennels." I climbed the steep stairs to my crow's nest and surveyed the area I hadn't seen for days. I took the first of a series of photos looking across the park between my house and our neighborhood community center. The Atlantic Ocean was just visible in the distance. I thought it might be useful later for identifying vehicles parked on the square at odd times. I should have been a private eye.

The forensic lab notified me that testing was complete on the sample I had submitted. Allen and I went together to get the report. The lab was in a tiny one-story building in a research park in Norfolk. We were taken to an office where a technician explained the report they were giving me. She blushed sweetly when she saw Allen again. I suspected Allen had actually cleaned up for this visit.

"The saliva we picked up is canine and from a female dog. Breed: bichon frise. The red stains are human blood, Caucasian male, haplogroup, yadda yadda . . ." She lost me on the alphabet of genetics, and I wondered what else we could learn from this analysis.

"There's no way you can give me a name, I suppose."

"No. Even if we could, I would need to notify the man before I told you."

"What if he has a criminal record?"

"For that, we have to put it through CODIS, and the police or other law enforcement need to do that."

I recognized the name CODIS as referring to the national DNA databank maintained by the FBI. All I could do now, I realized, was to make a copy for myself and then give the original report to the police. "Can you tell me the age of the female bichon frise?"

"No, sorry. DNA doesn't tell us age."

Dumb question.

Allen looked at me as if he had lost a bit of respect for my intelligence.

We left with a report that I hoped could someday be used in court.

CHAPTER TEN

The next week passed peacefully, and I was considering the possibility that it was all over. I hoped that Claude Raper had given up harassing me. The police were waiting to find out if the DNA analysis from the lab matched any known criminal in the FBI's data bank. The first nip of autumn was in the air. I started a new book.

Through the east window in my crow's nest, I trained my binoculars on the road that ringed the grassy square between my street and the community center. I had kept up my little project of taking frequent pictures of this scene to make a record of vehicles that frequented the neighborhood. I could read license plates of cars within fifty yards or so.

While taking up my morning watch, I spotted Allen's van with his distinctive logo on the side. It was parked at the far left of my camera range, almost out of my sight. Why hadn't he parked in front of my house? The pavement there was empty. And where was Allen? I was not aware that he knew anyone else on my street. Maybe a new client? Who, on my street, had or needed a service dog? The longer I stood there, binoculars scanning that part of the block, the stranger it seemed. And why had he not come to my house? Even if he did have a new client on this street, he could at least drop in to see me.

I couldn't see through his windshield because of the sun's angle, so I couldn't tell if anyone was in the van or not.

My mystery writer's imagination kicked in and almost stopped my heart. What if Allen was stalking me? What if he and

Claude Raper had been in this together all along? Give her a service dog, concoct a story about a runaway, let her rescue it, give her time to bond with both dogs, kidnap one and . . . this made absolutely no sense and, like most of my brain farts, had to be discarded immediately. I descended the spiral staircase to my office on the second floor, grabbed a sweater and joined my dogs in the front yard.

"Kim! Trey! What are you doing?" I ran to the fence and found they were digging holes. Both dogs had already managed to scratch out holes at the base of the fence—holes almost big enough for them to slip under.

Trey turned and looked at me briefly, then went back to work, digging like a maniac. I started to grab them both up and dump them in the house, but thought better of it. I wanted to find out why they were doing this. They had never done it before. I stepped up to the gate and flipped up the iron latch.

I saw Allen coming toward me at a run.

Trey tried to crowd through beside me, and Kim squeezed her slender body under the fence through the hole she had made. I nudged Trey back with my foot and tried to push the gate closed.

"Did you see where he went?" Allen shouted as he ran toward me.

"Where *who* went?"

"Raper. He was parked right here," Allen said, now standing on the sidewalk outside my fence. "I was watching him watching you, but he drove off. I saw you looking through your binoculars, and he must have seen you, too."

I felt the gate vibrate beneath my hand. Trey squeezed through the opening and, at the same moment, Kim emerged from the hole she had dug beneath the fence. Both dogs ran across the street and into the park. They streaked across the grass with purpose, as if they knew where they were going.

"Help!" I screamed. "They'll be killed!"

The park was surrounded by a street used by everyone in our neighborhood. Service vehicles passed up and down often and in both directions. My dogs knew nothing about traffic. There was no way I could catch them on foot.

"What can we do?" I grabbed Allen by one arm, demanding an idea, a solution, something, as if he had some secret knowledge about rounding up wayward dogs. I gazed out across the park and saw two white spots crossing the road near the northeast corner of the park. Beyond the street lay an untended stand of live oak trees, their branches bent westward due to prevailing winds off the ocean.

Allen took off down the sidewalk, running for his van. If he was going to chase the dogs in his van, I would chase them on foot. I ran diagonally across the grassy park, leaping over a sandbox all the neighbors had chipped in to build. I ran to the spot where I thought Kim and Trey had crossed the street, and paused. Never in my life had I had a stronger desire to hear something. Anything. Barking? A car motor? Human voices? But here I stood, in perfect silence, not knowing what to do next.

Allen's van approached from the direction of the community center. He turned left and stopped in the street. He hopped out of the van, waving his arms and pointing toward the live oaks.

I crossed the street and headed for the trees, but now what? Which way?

I studied the trees in front of me. The leaves and branches were no help, but the ground—there was my roadmap. Broken twigs, trodden leaves, even a small tuft of white fur caught on a fallen branch. It was as if my eyes were working extra hard to make up for the sounds I was missing. I followed the faint trail, looking down and around for clues. I felt a hand on my shoulder and turned to see Allen. He pointed straight ahead. Could he hear barking?

We took off together and, no more than thirty yards ahead, there were my dogs. I have never laughed so hard.

Trey stood there, barking so vigorously his front feet bounced up and down. Kim was hanging by her teeth, a foot off the ground, and her teeth were firmly planted in the seat of Claude Raper's pants as he hung, sloth-style, from a branch. Her little body twisted back and forth like a pit bull on a knotted rope.

We waited among the live oaks until the police arrived. This time, we got both the good cop and the bad cop together. I was thankful that Allen could negotiate and explain the situation better than I could with my inability to watch more than one pair of lips. They were all talking at the same time. At length.

Officer Hawkin said to Allen and me, "Do you wish to press charges?"

Claude Raper stood a little removed from the four of us, trying to hide his bare backside. A flap of denim hung down, exposing a lily-white buttock.

"You damn straight, we want to press charges," Allen said.

I grabbed Kim up in my arms. "You got him, baby girl. You got him!"

CHAPTER ELEVEN

Over the next couple of months, the Humane Society, veterinarians, and various state representatives descended on the Holly Grove Kennels and determined that it was in violation of so many regulations, it only made sense to shut it down. But when Claude Raper stood trial on charges of arson, setting fire to an occupied residence, the case ran into a bit of trouble.

The plaster cast of the footprint the fire marshal found near the dryer vent could not be connected to Raper. I suspected he had discarded the boots he was wearing that night.

The bloody cloth was evidence that he had been on my property at some time, but when?

This was where that cigarette butt saved the day. With all the documentation I had insisted upon, plus the dated photo and the obvious fact the item had not been rained on, Raper's DNA on the butt nailed him. His sentence of ten years in the slammer made the continued operation of the business where Trey began life and from which Kim escaped, a moot point.

Claude Raper's records, if you can dignify them with that label, were so sloppily maintained—in pencil and only on water-soaked paper—they were of no use to authorities. But I sort of wish he had kept better records. I can't help wondering if Kim could be Trey's mother.

THE END

A SHOT IN THE BARK

By Teresa Inge

When Catt Ramsey, owner of the Woof-Pack Dog Walkers hires an ex-con as her handy-man to help around the property and construct a Doggie Festival in her backyard, she stumbles upon two thefts and a dead neighbor. When accused of the murder, Catt solicits the help of her sister, Em, family friend Jonathan Ray, and her pups Cagney and Lacey to solve the mystery.

––––––––––––

TERESA INGE grew up reading Nancy Drew mysteries. Today, she doesn't carry a rod like her idol, but she hotrods. Love of reading mysteries and writing professional articles led to writing short fiction and novellas. She is president of Sisters in Crime Mystery by the Sea Chapter and author of short mysteries in Virginia is for Mysteries, 50 Shades of Cabernet, Coastal Crimes: Mysteries by the Sea, To Fetch a Thief, To Fetch a Scoundrel, *and* Murder by the Glass.

Website: www.TeresaInge.com

CHAPTER ONE

Catt Ramsey grabbed a bag of dog treats from the Woof-Pack Dog Walker's supply closet. She spun around and came face-to-face with Beau Whitaker. "Oh-mi-god!" She grabbed her chest. "You scared the holy crap out of me."

Beau, a handyman she had recently hired to fix things around her business, was a handsome, stockily built man with a large measure of southern charm. He smiled. "Sorry, darling. Didn't mean to startle you."

"It's okay. What's up?"

Catt's Yorkshire terriers Cagney and Lacey stood behind Beau, growling. Catt released a heavy breath and closed the door. "Hush." She waved her hand toward the dogs and turned her focus to Beau.

"This." Beau held up a green rope that usually held the key to the storage shed. They kept it hanging on a hook by the shed for easy access.

"Where's the key?" Catt asked.

Beau shrugged. "Dunno."

Catt scooted around him in the narrow hallway and walked to her desk. She set the treats down. Cagney and Lacey followed, their noses sniffing the aroma from the bag.

"Okay you two. Here you go." She pulled two treats out of the bag. The dogs eagerly took them and headed back to their beds, no longer interested in Beau.

Catt opened the desk drawer and fished around for the spare key she kept there. "It's my only spare." She handed it to Beau.

"Please don't lose it."

"I need to get some tools. I'll bring it back."

As Beau exited the door, Em entered.

"Beau sure was in a hurry," Em said.

"Yeah. He's finishing the runway for the doggie festival." Catt referred to the dog event scheduled in two days to help animals and promote her business.

Em headed to the coffee pot and poured herself a cup. She leaned against the counter and took a long sip. "I don't trust him."

"Beau? He's okay," Catt said.

"He's an ex-con." Em took another sip.

"True. But he's rehabilitated and deserves a second chance. Plus, Beau said he only drove the get-away car and was not involved in the robbery."

"All cons say that."

Catt picked up an envelope from the corner of her desk. "Here's the rent check." She handed it to Em.

"I'm glad you're paying on time now," Em teased.

Catt and Em had not always gotten along, but two years ago when Catt had lost her corporate events planning job and discovered her husband's cheating ways, Em let Catt move into her cottage above her garage in Virginia Beach. The space also served as home base for the Woof-Pack Dog Walkers. "Now that the business is growing, thanks to you joining the team, we can serve more clients. More clients means more money, which means I can now pay my bills on time."

"Everything worked out." Em rinsed her cup in the sink. "Speaking of clients, we have a full schedule today."

The door swung open. Samantha "Sammy" Norris, Catt's other dog walker, sashayed in like a welcomed summer breeze. She pushed her sunglasses into her long curls and plopped in the chair. Sammy had been working for Woof-Pack for the past year, juggling her work schedule while attending college.

"Good morning," Sammy said. "I see Beau is getting everything ready for Saturday. Looks like a real doggie park."

"Thanks." Catt grabbed three folders from her desk. "Since

we have a busy day ahead us, let's get started on reviewing things." She handed one folder to Em, one to Sammy, and kept one for herself. "You'll find the event schedule, a map, and a volunteer list. The first page in the packet is the schedule which runs ten to two."

Em flipped through the folder. "Which events did you decide on?"

They'd brainstormed so many great ideas, but the small yard limited what they could host. "Four. The doggie dash, Frisbee toss, doggie ice cream eating contest, and Pawject Runway where each dog will walk the runway in its best outfit. Sammy, do you have the music ready?" Catt asked.

"Yep. It's all set. The playlist will stream throughout the day. 'Who Let the Dogs Out' will play during Pawject Runway's red carpet," Sammy added.

"Thanks. Oh. I just thought of something else. Em, did you get the event permit?"

"It's right here." Em handed Catt an envelope.

"Thanks." Catt reviewed the permit and placed it in her folder. "The next page is a map of where each event is set up. We want everyone to experience it like a small doggie park. A welcome station, which includes a pet-related vendor and an adoption shelter rep, will be on the veranda. To the far right, you'll see the food and beverage station, and behind the oak tree we'll place a portable restroom. Oh…and Beau is putting up entrance and exit signs to guide the guests and their pets through the event."

The group viewed the map.

"Amazing use of space." Sammy pointed toward the map.

Catt nodded.

"How many people are coming?" Em asked.

"Fifty plus." Catt said. "It will be open house."

"Will food and beverages be available throughout the entire day?" Sammy asked.

"Yes. The sub shop around the corner is donating sandwiches, subs, and chips."

"That's awesome." Sammy fished through her purse and

pulled out her phone.

Catt continued. "Throughout the event, the emcee will be announcing raffle winners. All prizes have been donated by local businesses."

"Wow. You've done a great job with the budget," Sammy remarked.

"On the last page, you'll see the volunteer list. They'll arrive at eight. Bagels, croissants, muffins, OJ, water, and coffee will be on hand for them."

"All donated?" Em asked.

"Of course."

Em ran her finger down the list. "Are there enough volunteers to cover all four events?"

"Yes. You both will act as floaters." Catt pointed toward the paper.

"Floaters?" A quizzical look appeared on Em's face.

"If volunteers need to take a break, you can relieve their station or if guests need help, you can assist them throughout the day."

"So, we're gophers?" Em smirked.

"Something like that," Catt said.

Em pushed the paper to the side. "Ava Cartwright is volunteering?"

Ava was a client that they all knew.

"Yeah. Why?" Catt inquired.

"She's bossy, and her dogs are spoiled rotten," Em said.

"Look, we can't be picky since we need all of the volunteers on the list." Catt walked to the counter and pulled a shirt from a box. "Here's the volunteer t-shirts I picked up yesterday. What do you think?"

"The light blue Woof-Pack dog logo is nice against the gray shirt," Sammy said.

"I love it," Em added.

Catt folded the shirt and placed it back in the box. "We can give them to the volunteers when they arrive." Catt viewed the list and turned toward Em. "Did you pick up the paper products?"

"I left them by the shed. I couldn't find the key to put them away, though."

"The key went missing this morning. I just gave Beau the spare. I'm sure he'll put everything away."

"Where would the key have gone?"

Catt shrugged.

"I'm sure it'll turn up. Anyway, here's the Post-it list where I ticked off everything I purchased." Em handed the list to Catt.

"And here's the receipt for the supplies." Em handed Catt the paper. "It came to three hundred dollars."

Catt placed it in her folder.

"I just looked the weather up for Saturday on my phone. Mid-eighties," Sammy said.

"Good to know. Everyone will need to stay hydrated. There will be plenty of water on hand." Catt glanced at the list again. "That covers everything."

"Well if that's all...I need to walk Ava's dogs since she likes punctuality. But I would rather just punch her. Too-da-loo!" Em laughed and headed out the door and down the stairs.

"Guess she's not too fond of Ava." Sammy approached Catt. "I need to head out as well. I have several walks scheduled."

After Sammy left, Catt sat at her desk and opened her laptop. She emailed the volunteers the activities list, t-shirt info, and assigned roles. After downing half a turkey sandwich, she dusted off her hands and glanced at the dog walking schedule. Sammy had been the one to set up the app for her, enabling them to update the schedule and share information in real time. She smiled, proud that the schedule was up-to-date and everything covered.

Beau entered the office with the spare key in hand. "Where do you want it?"

Catt extended her hand. Beau passed her the key and she slipped it into her pocket. She made a mental note to have a spare made later today.

"I finished the runway. Wanna take a look?" Beau asked.

Catt nodded and closed her laptop. She picked up Em's Post-it note with the items ticked off and followed Beau outside with Cagney and Lacey in tow.

The backyard had been turned into a small doggie fairground. A long, raised walkway topped with a strip of red outdoor carpet stretched along the property line. A perfect venue for the dogs to strut their stuff. A circular steel gate surrounded the area from where participants could watch the show.

Beau strutted down the runway.

Catt laughed. "Perfect."

"Thanks, darling. I think so too."

She cringed every time Beau called her darling, especially since she was his boss. But she was trying to get to know him better in their employer/employee relationship.

Beau led Catt to the doggie dash. Markers identified how far each dog ran during the dash. To the right, a small space was squared off for the Frisbee toss, and further down were two tables and coolers for the doggie ice cream eating contest.

"It's compact, but it works," Catt said.

"I made good use of the space." Beau waved his hand toward the yard.

They walked toward the shed. Catt pulled the key and Post-it from her pocket and unlocked the door. "Here's the supplies that Em bought for Saturday. We'll need to put them out first thing that morning." She did a comparison to her list.

"I can take care of that," Beau offered.

Her inventory included boxes of animal treats, toys, and trinkets she used for the business. To the right, cases of bottled water sat on shelves by the outdoor tables. "Bottled water is missing."

Beau turned toward Catt. "Really?"

Catt walked to the shelf. She placed her hand on the cases and counted them. "Looks like five cases are missing."

"Are you sure?"

"Didn't you stack ten the other day?"

"I believe so. Maybe Em or Sammy used them."

"They didn't mention it. I'll check the inventory sheet when I go back in the office." Catt paused. "While we're here, can you grab two tables and I'll grab two."

"Sure." Beau grabbed two tables and handed them to Catt before grabbing two more. "Where do you want them?"

"On the veranda. Follow me."

Catt placed two in the front for the welcome and check in table. "You can put the other two side by side for the vendor and adoption rep."

"How many people you got coming over?" Beau leaned against a wooden column.

"Around fifty or so clients, potential clients, friends, and neighbors."

"I can be here early Saturday to put out the products and make last-minute adjustments."

"I appreciate it."

"What about the restroom?"

"It's being delivered on Friday. Can you handle that when it arrives?"

"Sure. But that's for humans. What about the dogs?"

Catt laughed. "By the oak tree. I made signs for everyone to scoop their poop. Bags will be available on a table."

"You thought of everything."

"By the way. Do you want to bring your dog?"

"Sure. Duke would love to be a part of it."

An alert appeared on Catt's phone. "I have an appointment to walk a dog. Gotta run."

"Okay. I'll see you in the morning. If you need anything before then, text me."

CHAPTER TWO

Catt headed up the stairs to her office and opened her laptop to check the inventory list. According to the last order, ten cases of bottled water had been delivered and stored in the shed. She closed her laptop and leashed Cagney and Lacey since she often walked them with Grayson.

She walked the two blocks to The Loft, six-story, contemporary building where many of the Woof-Pack clients lived. It never failed to impress her when she first caught sight of it. It overlooked the beach and boardwalk and was home to many wealthy residents.

She swiped her key card and headed to the sixth floor to Brock Randall's apartment. She let herself in. Grayson, a well-groomed gray poodle with a pom pom tail, rushed toward Cagney and Lacey in the foyer to sniff them. "Hi boy," Catt said.

The luxurious apartment was decorated in a coastal chic design of soft blue hues, linen fabrics, distressed woods, nautical prints, and coral shells. The luminous finishes gave a calm tranquility to the space.

Brock stumbled in from the hallway, scraping his feet on the carpet. He looked like he had just rolled out of bed and thrown on a pair of wrinkly sweats. This trust-fund baby and former city council member usually was a fashion plate and heartthrob for every single woman within a fifty-foot radius.

Startled at Brock's appearance, Catt's eyes widened since he was always fashionable. "Didn't you have a meeting this afternoon?"

"I'm not feeling well so I didn't go." Brock rubbed his stomach.

"Can I get you something?"

"No, thanks. I heard Grayson bark, so I got out of bed. Are you going for a walk?"

"Yes. Get some rest. I'll be quiet when I return him. Oh, by the way. Are you still bringing Grayson to the doggie fair on Saturday?"

"If I feel better, we'll be there."

Catt made her way to the boardwalk with Cagney, Lacey, and Grayson. She enjoyed her stroll, even if she did have to dodge slow-moving tourists and fast-moving runners, many accompanied by leashed dogs. The ocean breeze gave a soothing comfort to her and the dogs against the June heat and humidity.

Catt approached Em, who was walking Chopper and Ollie, Ava Cartwrights two beagle-terrier mixes. "How are they doing today?"

"Well, this is round two. After I walked them this morning, Ava asked me to walk them again this afternoon since she had to run errands. But at least they're listening to me today. I received specific instructions from Ava not to walk them too fast or overexpose them to the heat since 'her babies' can't take it." Em used finger quotes to emphasize her words.

Cagney, Lacey, and Grayson sniffed their two new friends.

"Well, just keep them hydrated since the humidity *is* up today." Catt held the dog's leashes in one hand while tightening her ponytail with her other hand. She petted Chopper and Ollie. Ollie extended her paw toward her. "Aww...what a good girl." Chopper remained fixated on the dogs.

"I see from the schedule you have two more to walk after Chopper and Ollie." Catt checked the schedule on her phone.

"Yeah. Then I'm done for the day. Jonathan Ray and I are going straight to the beach to do some metal detecting." Jonathan Ray, a childhood friend, had dated Em when they were teenagers. They had rekindled their relationship after they bumped into each other during a murder investigation of one of Catt's clients two years ago. Since then, the two have discovered the fine art of metal detecting together.

"Is Jonathan Ray still coming to the doggie fair?" Catt asked.

"Yep. And I know what you're thinking. He already said he can be a gopher."

Catt laughed. "You know me too well, sis."

"By the way, was everything okay with the set up?" Em asked.

"Yes. Beau did a great job. He'll be there early tomorrow to put out the supplies. Hey, there is one thing. Five cases of bottled water are missing from the shed. Did you see them?"

"No. How do you know they're missing?"

"When Beau and I were in the shed today, the cases didn't stack to the top shelf. I distinctly remember when the order came in, Beau had piled them on top of each other."

"I haven't. But it's strange they're gone. Do you think Beau took them?"

"Why would he take them? He's the one who stacked it for me."

"Exactly. And he had the spare key. Plus, do we really know that the key actually fell off the rope like he said?"

"Beau didn't steal the key or the water."

Em frowned. Chopper and Ollie tugged their leashes. "I think they're ready to go. Let me know what you find out about the water." Em headed down the boardwalk.

CHAPTER THREE

Catt's phone pinged and she checked the alert. Sammy added an additional slot. She sent her a quick text to see if she needed help. Sammy texted back that she had it covered.

Thirty minutes later, Catt returned Grayson to Brock's apartment. She entered the apartment quietly and hung his leash back on the wall.

Catt toyed with her phone while waiting for the elevator. Rhea Lucas Prentiss, a lady as fancy as her name and one of Catt's clients, strode nearer with Pritzie tucked safely in the crook of her arm next to her oversized Coach bag. Pritzie, a spunky Pomeranian Spitz, yipped her greeting.

"Well, hello Catt. I see you've got the two troublemakers with you." Rhea smirked. "What are you all up to today?"

"I walked Brock's dog, Grayson."

"Oh…him." Rhea curled her lip. "He's such a snob. How *do* you stand him?"

Catt smiled. She categorized Rhea and Brock in the same snobbish category. But as her clients, she had to get along with both, even though Rhea disliked Brock immensely since they broke up.

The elevator doors opened. "After you." Catt held her hand out and boarded the elevator with Cagney and Lacey after Rhea. Catt pushed the lobby button. "Are you and Pritzie still coming to the doggie fair on Saturday?"

"Of course. I got Pritzie the cutest outfit for the fashion show."

"Well…it's not exactly a fashion show but more of a best-dressed."

Rhea grabbed Pritzie's paw and pointed it toward Catt. She spoke in a baby voice. "We plan to win that fashion show!"

The door opened. Catt stepped out with the dogs. "Well, I'll see you Saturday. I'm glad you and Pritzie will be there." Catt took long strides from the elevator and didn't look back. She could only tolerate Rhea in small doses.

Before heading to the cottage, Catt stopped at a local hardware store just past 17th Street for a new spare key. The missing key still bothered her. It shouldn't have just slipped off the rope. She wanted to trust Beau. Afterall, his background check had come back clean. But like Em had pointed out, he had a past.

Back at the office, she sat her bag on the desk then filled Cagney and Lacey's water bowls. While they lapped up the water, she grabbed the rope off her desk and secured the new key to it. "Let's go out back," she yelled to the dogs. The three headed out the door and down the stairs.

Catt walked around the grounds, searching for the missing key. Cagney and Lacey did their business on the back of the property. The key had to be here somewhere. She was convinced that Beau did not take it for the sole purpose of stealing water. Who does that?

Cagney and Lacey approached her. "Help mama find the key," she said as if they understood. After walking the grounds, the attempt was futile.

She switched her focus toward the fair. Even though she was not charging admission, the fair would still bring in donations for local shelters. Jonathan Ray had set up a giving page and registration on Catt's website. It would also bring in new clients for her business.

When she turned toward the shed, her eye caught the door ajar. She walked closer and pushed it open. The storage shed was completely empty. She blinked, to make sure her eyes weren't tricking her. All the supplies were gone from the shelves. Water, paper products, animal treats, toys, and trinkets.

She put her hand to her mouth. "Oh-mi-god! We've been robbed!"

CHAPTER FOUR

What time did you discover the items missing, Ms. Ramsey?" Jax Monroe, a Virginia Beach detective, held a pen and notepad in his hand.

"About three thirty." Catt rubbed her forehead.

"Besides everything in the shed, are there any other items missing on the property?"

"Uh...not that I know of. But it's actually not my property."

"Whose property is it?"

"My sister's. I live and work above the cottage. I store stuff for my business in the shed."

"Are you having an event here?" The detective pointed his pen toward the runway.

"Yes. A doggie fair on Saturday. I run a dog-walking business here. I have my business license and permits."

"I see." As he scribbled notes on the pad, another officer approached. Detective Monroe turned away from Catt. The men talked in low tones. Turning toward Catt, Detective Monroe continued, "Seems we have a witness. Your next-door neighbor said a stocky Caucasian man was on your property earlier. Do you know who that might be?"

Catt glanced over the detective's shoulder. Richard Boykins, the neighborhood, watch and gossip, stood in his backyard pretending to prune his rose bushes.

"That was probably my handyman," Catt said in almost a whisper.

"What's his name?"

Catt let out a heavy sigh and had an internal battle with herself about telling on her maintenance guy. She paused and tried to keep her voice from quivering. "Beau Whitaker."

"Do you have a contact number for Mr. Whitaker?"

"Uh…yes." She pulled her phone and gave him the number.

"I need you to make a list of the missing items." He handed her the pen and notepad.

Catt headed to the shed to start the list.

Monroe followed.

Em and Jonathan Ray approached her and the detective. "What's going on?" Em had a concerned look on her face. Jonathan Ray stood silent.

"And you are?" Detective Monroe spoke before Catt could respond.

Em placed her hands on her curvy hips. "I'm Em Ramsey, and I own the property. This is my boyfriend Jonathan Ray."

"I'm detective Jax Monroe. Someone got into the shed and stole your sister's pet supplies."

Em's mouth flew open. "What?"

"Yeah. The door was open when I got back from walking the dogs."

"How did they break into the shed?" Em asked.

"It doesn't appear to be an actual break in. It's more like the door was left unlocked," the detective suggested.

"What do you mean?" Catt asked.

"Seems the door was either left unlocked or someone used a key. Who has a key to the shed?"

"I do." Catt held up the green rope with the shiny new key. "We keep it hanging on the shed. But the key went missing this morning."

The detective frowned. "Am I missing something? There's a key on that rope."

Catt agreed. "I had another one made earlier today. I was out here looking for the original on the ground when I discovered the shed door open."

"I see," the detective said. "So the key was accessible to everyone?"

Catt smiled and shrugged. She wanted to add that the only people who had access to the property had access to the key, but she held her tongue.

"Didn't you say there were five cases of bottled water missing when you were in the shed earlier today?" Em asked.

"What happened earlier?" Detective Monroe asked.

"When Beau, my handyman and I got some tables out of the shed earlier for the fair, they were missing. Afterward I checked my inventory and confirmed it."

"So, we have two thefts?" the detective asked.

"Uh…yes," Catt said.

The detective wiped his brow from the heat. "Okay from the start. Who has a key to the shed?"

Catt worried that the detective did not believe her. "I do. And there was one spare which was missing from the rope, which I replaced."

"So, the other key is still missing?"

"Yes."

"Any chance the handyman or someone else has it?"

"No."

"Any chance someone could have taken the supplies on your behalf?"

"No."

"Did you lock the shed behind you earlier today?" the officer asked.

"Yes. I locked it."

"Okay. So, go ahead and take inventory of what is missing. I'll call Mr. Whitaker," the detective said.

Catt entered the shed. Em and Jonathan Ray followed. "I thought you two were going metal detecting," Catt said.

"I had to come home to get another pair of shoes," Em said. "But what were you thinking in hiring a convict?" Em asked in an accusatory tone.

"Look. I was trying to give him a chance. Plus, we don't know that Beau had anything to do with it." Catt pushed her hair off her shoulders from the heat.

"You okay?" Em asked.

"I'm overwhelmed with the fair, and now this." Tears fell down Catt's cheek.

"It's okay." Em patted Catt's back.

She placed her hand on the shelf. "Just about everything is gone. All the paper products you purchased. The water." Catt rubbed her forehead. "I can't even think right now. It's going to take time to figure out what is missing and replace all of this."

"Since I gave you the receipt this morning for the paper products and you have an inventory of everything else. I'll go pull that information off the computer to give to the detective," Em suggested.

"That's perfect," Catt said. One less thing on her to do list.

Jonathan Ray stepped closer as Em headed out the door. "I'm sorry this happened."

Catt forced a smile. "I don't understand why someone would take my supplies."

"What about Sammy? Did you ask her?"

"I texted her earlier and she didn't know anything about it."

Em returned with the list of missing supplies and gave it to Detective Monroe. Catt and Jonathan Ray gathered around them.

"Tell me. Do you have a surveillance camera on the property?" he asked Em.

"Yes."

"Any chance you can view the footage and send it to me?" Detective Monroe jotted in his notebook.

"Sure."

The detective handed her a business card. "Here's my contact info."

Beau entered the backyard. Everyone stared at him.

"Can I help you?" Detective Monroe said.

"Um. I'm Beau Whitaker. Someone called me to come over."

"Yes. I spoke to you on the phone. Thanks for coming so quickly."

Beau nodded. "What's going on?"

"There's been a burglary," the detective said.

"What?"

"Pet supplies and cases of water were stolen from the shed today. I understand you were working in the backyard?"

"Uh. Yeah." Beau cut his eyes toward Catt. "I was setting up everything for Saturday.

"And you and Ms. Ramsey were in the shed today when she discovered the missing water?"

"Yes."

"You know anything about that?"

"No. I don't know what happened to it."

The officer jotted notes on his pad. "What time did you leave the property?"

Beau ran his hand through his wavy hair. "Around two something."

The detective glanced at his notes. "Do you know what happened to the key that was on the green rope?"

"No."

"Was there anyone else on the property when you were working?"

"Just me. But Catt was in the cottage working." Beau hesitated. "Come to think of it, when I finished, the dogs next door were barking like crazy."

"Are you referring to Richard Boykins' house next door?" The detective pointed behind Beau.

"Yes."

"Was he in the yard?"

"No."

"Did you see anyone else?"

"No."

"I don't have any further questions. But I have your number if something comes up."

Beau turned toward Catt. "How are you doing?"

"I've been better." She waved her hand for Beau to follow her to the shed, leaving Em and Jonathan Ray to speak to the detective.

He twitched as he entered the empty shed. "What's with all the gray spots?" He rested his arm on the shelf.

"They dusted for fingerprints." Catt rubbed her head. "I

hope we can recover since the guests will be arriving. Plus, I'm short on funds."

"When did this happen?"

"Sometime between the time you left and the time I returned from walking Brock's dog."

"Who did this?"

"That's the million-dollar question," Catt said.

"Maybe it's someone in the neighborhood?"

"Maybe."

"We've been working on the fair all week. Do you think someone got upset over it?"

"But why would they take the water and supplies? Why wouldn't they have taken the fair decorations and games?" Catt asked.

"I don't know."

"And how did they get them without busybody Boykins next door not seeing them?"

Detective Monroe approached the shed. "Ms. Ramsey. I let your sister know we have done everything we can here. She will send me the surveillance footage. I've also asked Mr. Boykins to check his cameras to see if they captured anything. But in the meantime, I'll file a report and will be in touch."

"Thank you very much," Catt said.

Catt, Em, Beau, and Jonathan Ray huddled near the shed. No one said a word until the detective had disappeared around the corner.

Richard Boykins leaned over the fence as he pruned his roses, but it couldn't have been more obvious he was listening to their conversation.

"It's so weird how this happen in broad daylight," Jonathan Ray said.

"Yeah. I'm thinking the same thing," Catt said. She tapped her finger against her lip. "But you know what puzzles me the most?"

"What?" Em said as the rest looked toward Catt.

"That Richard didn't see what happened. Usually things don't get past him. They would have needed a cart or wheelbarrow to carry out all the supplies."

"I did notice the police looking for trampled grass and tire prints," Jonathan Ray added.

"Between that and the videos, hopefully they'll find out who did it," Catt said.

Em crossed her arms in a defiant stance. "So, Beau. Since Richard didn't see anyone that leaves you. And with your, uh, background, did you take the supplies?"

Beau's eyes crossed. "I didn't have anything to do with it. And if you don't believe me, then maybe it's best that I don't work here." He stormed off, jumped in his truck, and squealed tires on the road.

"Good grief!" Catt wondered if Beau would be back.

CHAPTER FIVE

Friday morning Catt jumped out of bed when the sun's rays poked through her curtains. She made an espresso to give her the charge she needed to walk Pritzie and Grayson. To save time, she would walk them together even though Rhea detested Brock.

She headed to the sixth floor of The Loft and retrieved Pritzie. Next, the duo made their way down the hall to Brock's apartment to get Grayson. Catt chose the order, so Rhea wouldn't know that her baby was hanging out with Brock's dog. Pritzie was as high maintenance as her dog mom.

She entered Brock's apartment. Grayson greeted her and Pritize at the door. She leashed him and off the three went to the boardwalk.

As Catt walked the dogs, she enjoyed the slight breeze off the ocean which gave her time to clear her mind about Beau, the theft, and her neighbor Richard Boykins.

While walking toward the King Neptune Statue located at the entrance of Neptune Park, Ava Cartwright, her husband James, and dogs Ollie and Chopper approached her. "Hi, Catt and pups!" Ava was bright and cheery this morning.

The four dogs sniffed each other.

"You're out early. How are you?"

"Doing great. I decided to walk the pups myself since Em overheated them yesterday."

Catt frowned hearing this news. "Are they okay?"

"They're fine," James interrupted.

Ava rolled her eyes at James. "Of course, they're fine.

However, when they returned from their afternoon walk yesterday, they were exhausted."

"It *was* warm yesterday. But I saw them with Em on the boardwalk, and they were doing well. Maybe they were tired."

"Maybe," Ava said. She glanced at the dogs. "I see you have Brock and Rhea's dogs today. Do they get along?"

"Perfectly."

"I'm surprised, since Rhea can't stand Brock."

Ava is nosy. "Well the pups like each other."

"I see. Oh, I got your email about volunteering tomorrow. I'll be there early, and James will come along later with Chopper and Ollie."

"Thanks, James." Catt smiled.

He nodded.

Pritzie jumped up and down. "Looks like she's ready to go. I'll see you tomorrow." Catt headed down the boardwalk and back to The Loft to drop off the dogs.

When Catt returned to her office, she waved at Beau in the backyard, modifying a few setups for tomorrow. He nodded without speaking. His cool reaction was probably due to the awkward accusation from Em toward him yesterday, when he'd denied taking the items. Although Catt believed him, she had to be realistic about the situation and his background. She set her things down and took care of some items for tomorrow. Em was in the house pulling the surveillance footage for the detective. Catt planned to stop at the store to repurchase the products. But first, she would check on Beau to make sure he was okay.

"Hi there." Catt approached Beau who stood by the shed.

"The porta john was just delivered." Beau didn't look at Catt.

She opened the door to the bathroom. "It looks good."

"I've seen worse." Beau smirked.

Catt decided to lighten the mood. She turned toward the runway. "I like how you moved the gate closer to the runway."

After an awkward silence, Beau responded. "Makes it easier for guests to stand near the rail and watch the show. Plus, the pathway is wider now to add extra space."

"Good thinking. I need to head out to restock supplies for tomorrow. Is there anything you need before I go?" Catt asked.

Beau shook his head.

"Uh…about yesterday. I know that was uncomfortable when Em questioned you about the theft."

Beau gave Catt a long stare. "Look. I get it. I'm the new guy with a criminal background so that makes me the prime suspect. But I want to be clear that I did not take anything from the shed. That's the honest truth. Why would I need cases of water and pet supplies? It's not even valuable."

Catt wanted to believe him since he had been forthcoming about his background, but she also needed to be cautious.

Cagney and Lacey started barking, taking her out of her thoughts.

"Excuse me. Excuse me." A woman walking a small dog approached from the back of the yard. "Are you Catt Ramsey?"

"Yes, ma'am. May I help you?" Catt asked.

"You're darn tootin' you can." She held the leash while resting her hands on her slim hips stuffed into a tight pair of jeans. "Are you missing a bunch of cups, plates, bottled water, pet toys and other stuff?"

Cagney and Lacey stood beside Catt, barking at the woman and her dog in their yard.

"Yes. Do you know where they are?"

"I sure do. After fixing myself a cup of coffee first thing this morning, I opened the front door to let Pookie here out and lo and behold…there they were! Red plastic plates, silverware, paper towels, boxes of treats and toys, bottled water, and red cups scattered across my front yard. It was like a red Solo cup explosion. Couldn't believe my own eyes. Even took an extra-large sip of coffee to make sure I wasn't seeing things."

The woman seemed familiar. "Where do you live, Ms…?" Catt asked.

"Two blocks over. My name is Vanessa Carlson."

"How did you know they belonged to me?"

"After the initial shock of seeing it all, I looked closer and printed on one of the boxes was Catt Ramsey, Woof-Pack Dog

Walkers and your address. Plus, some of the trinkets had your brand on them. There was also a Post-it attached to a cup with a list of supplies. Stuff that is now in my yard. I Googled your name. Your photo popped up, and I recognized it from my friend Richard, so here I am."

Catt must have left the Post-it on the supplies by accident when she was checking the list. "You know Richard?"

"Yes."

"But how did my stuff get in your yard?" Catt asked.

"That's what I was going to ask you."

Cagney and Lacey slowly approached Pookie. Vanessa loosened the leash around her hand, and the dogs walked toward each other.

"The supplies were stolen out of my shed yesterday. I filed a police report."

"I'm sorry to hear that, but what are you going to do about all that stuff?"

"I can come get it," Beau offered.

The woman scanned Beau's broad shoulders and handsome face. "Who are you?"

"The handyman. You want me to follow you?"

"Nope. I'm on foot."

"You and Pookie can ride with me in my truck," Beau said.

"Sure."

The dogs took off running around the yard.

"What is all this anyway?" Vanessa waved her hand toward the runway.

"We're having a doggie fair tomorrow. There will be lots of people, and dogs enjoying fun activities," Catt said.

"Oh really?" Vanessa asked.

"You're welcome to bring Pookie. It's from ten to two."

"I might do that," Vanessa said.

"Other neighbors will be here too," Beau added.

From the corner of Catt's eye, she caught Richard Boykins approaching with his dogs. Oh brother. Here comes trouble.

CHAPTER SIX

"Hi Vanessa," Richard said, almost tripping over himself to get next to the svelte woman in painted-on jeans.

"Hey there," she cooed. "If it isn't my old drinking buddy, Richard, who's always up for a good time. I was telling Catt here that I've known you for more years than either of us will admit to." Vanessa winked and blew the older man a kiss. "You'll never tell, right?"

"How do you two know each other?" Catt asked.

"We've been good friends for years." Vanessa smiled toward Richard.

Catt didn't even want to know what that was about. "Can I help you with something?" she asked Richard.

"It's more like, how can *I* help *you*?" He crossed his arms against his chest as his dogs greeted the other dogs.

"And how is that?"

"Detective Monroe asked me to check the footage from my surveillance cameras, and I let him know there was a small image on the film. The face was shaded with a big hoodie. It was too blurry to make out since my camera is cheap. But I sent him the video."

"Do you know what time that was?" Beau asked.

"It's timestamped around three thirty. Were you here then?"

"Uh...no. I left before that. But it must have been before Catt arrived." Beau motioned toward Catt.

"That's true. I arrived after that. Wow. That's crazy to think I could have run into the person stealing everything."

"Well, at least you don't have to restock," Beau said.

Richard glared at Beau. "The supplies were found?"

"They were dumped in Vanessa's yard."

"Who did it?" Richard asked.

Vanessa shrugged her shoulders. "Who knows? Probably teenagers. But Beau is coming to my house to get them."

"I can help." Richard stood tall and puffed out his chest.

"I have garbage bags in my truck," Beau said.

"Let me put my dogs in the house. Be right back." Richard led his dogs to the side garage door.

Catt was surprised that Richard was being helpful. Was he really trying to help or just get close to Vanessa?

Thirty minutes later a car door slammed, and Catt popped her head out the window. Beau and Richard unloaded the garbage bags full of the stolen items from the truck bed.

"Where do you want them?" Beau asked.

"What kind of shape are they in?" Catt asked.

"Like perfect."

"Let's put them back in the shed." Catt unlocked the door. "Put them back on the shelves please."

"I really appreciate you both hauling everything back for me."

"Anything else?" Richard asked.

"No. But since we're done, anyone up for a beer?" Catt offered.

"Just what I need on a Friday night," Beau said.

"Me, too," Richard said.

Richard walked home and brought his two shepherd mix dogs Max and Sheldon over, while Beau picked up Duke and brought him back.

The three drank a couple of beers on the veranda as the dogs played together.

"You coming to the fair tomorrow?" Catt asked Richard.

"Absolutely. I'm bringing these two knuckle-heads with me. Cheers to good neighbors." Richard raised his beer.

Beau sipped his beer. "So, what's Vanessa's story?"

"We dated on and off for years. She wanted to get married,

but I've been there done that. Fun to hang out with, but a little clingy."

Catt raised her eyebrows. She had no idea Richard had been married.

Beau glanced at Catt. "I get it. But I would get married again if I found the right girl."

Catt raised her eyebrows. Does he mean me? Not in a million years. She changed the subject. "Is Vanessa coming to the fair tomorrow?"

"She said she wouldn't miss it," Beau said.

"So, what's your story, man?" Richard asked Beau. "Where were you before you moved here?"

Beau pursed his lips. "I did something I'm not proud of. But I paid my dues and Catt gave me a second chance." He chugged his beer.

"And he's been doing a great job," Catt added.

"Sounds like you are on the right path." He paused. "Well, I think I'll call it a night," Richard said. "These two are ready for bed and, frankly so am I." He finished the rest of his beer, crushed the can, and threw it in the recycling bin.

"See you tomorrow. And thanks again," Catt said.

"Sure thing. I'll see you in the morning." Richard walked across the yard, and his dogs followed him into his backyard.

"I think this is the first time I've ever hung out or had a beer with Richard."

"Why is that?"

"Because I didn't like him. He was always getting in everyone's business in the neighborhood."

"Love thy neighbor." Beau held up his beer.

"Tomorrow is going to be a big day. Oh, by the way. I put the spare key back on the rope and hid it behind the grill on the veranda." Catt nodded toward the grill.

"Really?"

"Yeah. No one would ever know it was here. It would be too obvious if I hid it by the shed again. But it's there if you need it in the morning."

"You thought of all the details."

Catt leaned back in her chair. "It feels good to kick back and relax." Catt stretched her shoulders. Some of the tension from the workweek seemed to fade.

"Let me help you, darling." Beau leaned forward and placed his hands on her shoulders and rubbed them.

"You have the magic touch."

Beau smiled. "Glad you feel better."

Catt stared into Beau's brown eyes. His rugged good looks softened in the moonlight. There was low humidity, but Catt heated up inside.

He leaned forward and kissed her. She was hesitant to get involved. Beau was her employee. And she wasn't sure she wanted to jump into a new relationship since the one with Josh Harden had ended badly last year.

Cagney, Lacey, and Duke started barking, breaking Catt's train of thought.

Beau and Catt stood.

"What is it?"

"Over there, in Richard's bushes." Catt pointed toward the fence.

"Who's there?" Beau asked.

The dogs growled.

Beau crossed the yard in three strides. There was silence. He looked around then walked back toward Catt.

"Who is it?" Catt asked.

"It must have been that white cat that is always roaming the neighborhood."

"He gets Cagney and Lacey riled up," Catt added.

"Well. I guess everything is okay now. Duke and I should call it a night since we have to get up extra early tomorrow for the big day." Beau finished his beer.

"Thanks for everything," Catt said.

CHAPTER SEVEN

Saturday morning, Catt awoke earlier than expected. She was excited about the fair today, and still tingling after her kiss with Beau last night. After lying in bed with Cagney and Lacey, she got up, fed them, then jumped on the treadmill followed by a hot shower.

She grabbed the box of t-shirts for the volunteers off the counter in her office and headed to the welcome tables with Cagney and Lacey. Beau was already in the backyard with Duke, cleaning the coolers at the beverage station. "Morning," Beau said.

Catt set the box on the table and approached him. She petted Duke. "Thanks for coming out so early."

Duke moved closer to Cagney and Lacey and nudged them playfully.

"Sure thing. I wanted to make sure everything is stocked for today."

"Jonathan Ray and Richard will help you set up."

There was an awkward silence before Beau spoke. "About last night. I'm sorry if I overstepped my boundaries."

"We both needed to relax." Catt looked around. "Thanks for putting the paper products on the tables."

"Yep. Well…I better get back to it."

Catt took care of other tasks for the next hour and a half while Beau did final preps.

Em, Jonathan Ray, and Sammy entered the backyard.

"Gophers are here," Em yelled.

"I have the playlist ready. Where do you want the music set up?" Sammy asked.

"Over here on the veranda." Catt waved her hand in the air.

"Do you still want me to help Beau?" Jonathan Ray asked.

"Absolutely. Don't forget to grab your volunteer shirt from the table."

Jonathan Ray slipped the volunteer shirt over his shirt and walked toward Beau.

Sammy and Em grabbed their shirts. Sammy began setting up and testing the music.

"What do you need me to do, sister dear?" Em asked.

"Since the volunteers will be here soon, can you give them their shirts as they arrive and check their name off the volunteer list?"

"You got it."

"Then you and Sammy can be floaters throughout the day."

Catt yelled toward Sammy. "Did you clear the dog walking schedule for the day, even though most of our clients will be here?" Catt asked.

"All clear."

Catt grabbed the bagels, muffins, and croissants from her office and placed them on a table for the volunteers. A few minutes later, ten volunteers strolled into the yard and stood in line to get their t-shirt from Em and breakfast off the table.

Ava Cartwright bypassed the line and headed toward Catt. "Morning."

"Morning, Ava. Thanks for coming out to volunteer. You can pick up your t-shirt from Em and get breakfast." Catt waved her hand toward the line.

"I don't wait in lines." Ava glanced around the fair. "Nice setup. Reminds me of a park."

"Thanks. We've worked hard to pull it all together."

"I'm sure. Let me know where you need me."

"You can sit tight for a few minutes until I meet with the volunteers to review the schedule." Catt paused as the sandwiches, subs, and beverage delivery arrived. As Catt signed the delivery invoice, Beau and Jonathan Ray placed the items on the tables.

On second thought, Catt would put Ava to work since she refused to wait in line with the rest of the volunteers. "See the totes under the tables?" She pointed toward blue bins.

Ava nodded.

"Grab the utensils and place them by the trays on the tables. Oh…there are placard signs that need to go in front of each tray."

Ava started digging into the totes and pulling out the items.

After putting the last trays out, Beau and Jonathan Ray started filling the coolers with ice.

Catt made her way back to the welcome tables. She greeted the shelter rep and vendor and then welcomed the volunteers and reviewed logistics and assigned stations to them.

"This is Em and Sammy. They will relieve you for breaks and answer any questions you have. You can use the bathroom in my office and grab beverages from the fridge and sandwiches and snacks off the counter." Catt clapped her hands together. "If everyone can head to your station now and get ready. Guests will be here soon."

Catt rubbed her forehead. There was a lot of details to take care of. She felt like an orchestra conductor with all the moving parts. Thank goodness for the volunteers and for Beau supervising others. He showed great leadership during this time. She smiled. And last night.

Someone tapped Catt on her shoulder.

"Hi neighbor." Vanessa stood in a pair of tight white jeans and a low-cut blouse, Pookie by her side. "How's it going?"

"Great. I'm glad you came." Catt glanced at the time on her phone. "The fair will be starting soon."

"Have you seen Richard?" Vanessa asked.

"Uh…no. He said he would help set up this morning."

"I went to his house and knocked on the door but no answer. The dogs were barking."

"That's strange."

"I thought so, too." Vanessa shrugged. "Well, I'll see him when I see him."

Catt walked to the veranda to greet her guests. One by one, they entered the yard with their dogs in tow. Shepherds, Dobermans, chihuahuas, labs, and poodles, all dressed to the max in colorful tutu's, tuxedos, sundresses, and bling onesies.

"Hey there," a voice came from behind Catt. She turned.

"Brock, you made it. Are you feeling better?"

"Much."

Grayson ran towards Catt. "Hi, buddy. Aww...you both look cute."

Brock and Grayson were dressed in matching red bow ties.

Rhea and Pritzie pranced toward Catt and Brock. Rhea wore a pink silk blouse, white slacks, and a pink fascinator on her head. Pritzie wore a glitter pink tutu with a large pink bow on her head.

"Your two are dressed up," Catt said.

"I had her tutu custom made for the fashion show," Rhea said.

Catt had told Rhea it was not a fashion show...but whatever.

"How are you feeling?" Rhea asked Brock.

"Better. Thanks for bringing me soup. That was nice of you."

Rhea smiled. "Anytime."

Catt glanced at Brock and Rhea. "Are you two friends again, dare I ask?"

Rhea grabbed Brock's arm, and they began strolling around the fair with their dogs.

Catt shook her head. They're suited for each other.

She headed to the ice cream-eating contest. Volunteers sported their t-shirts and lined up each dog for the doggie ice cream contest and started the timed competition. Some dogs ate ice cream standing up, while others lay down on the grass to get better control of their ice cream cup. After a few minutes, the emcee announced a winner, and the next round of contestants lined up for their turn.

Satisfied the event was on track and participants were having fun, Catt headed to the Frisbee toss. Volunteers lined two to three dogs, side by side, threw Frisbees into the air and the dogs caught them. The tosses continued with dogs catching Frisbees.

Next, Catt walked to the doggie dash where dogs stood at the start line and then raced to the finish. First to arrive was declared the winner of that round. Catt stood by the marked area, talking to guests as the emcee announced giveaways throughout the day.

Catt glanced at Em leaning against the Pawject Runway rail. She walked over. "How's it going, sis?"

"Everyone seems to be enjoying themselves, except that annoying Ava. She has called me to this station four times. Says she can't work without multiple breaks. She keeps going up to the office to eat, drink, and cool off in the AC."

"How many breaks does she need?" Catt asked.

"A lot. I'm hanging around until she calls again. James brought the dogs, so they could walk the runway. Oh, look the music is starting." "Who Let the Dogs Out" began playing as each dog strutted their stuff down the red carpet.

A crowd gathered outside the circular rail that Beau had built.

Pritzie, Grayson, Pookie, Chopper, and Ollie finished the round. Five dogs could participate per round and whoever received the loudest clap from the audience was deemed the winner. After the music stopped and the crowd clapped, the emcee declared Pritzie the winner.

"I have to check on some things. Let me know if Ava gets too high maintenance." Catt trudged to the welcome station to help check in guests and talk to the vendor and shelter reps. Two dog adoptions occurred, as Catt's neighbors became pet parents of a beagle and a border collie. The vendor sold several hand-made pet items which would benefit the shelter. Catt was happy to hear the update. She turned just as Ava headed up the stairs to Catt's office. She finished checking in another guest and excused herself from the table.

"Can I help you with something?" Catt said to Ava as she entered her office.

Ava stood at Catt's desk with the drawer open. "Uh...sorry. I was just looking for something to write on. I need to make a reminder to myself to stop by the store later. I can't remember anything anymore."

"Oh sure. There are Post-it notes in the drawer. Pens are in the desk."

"Thanks."

Catt walked to the fridge to grab a bottled water. "Everything okay at your station?"

"Oh sure. Em has been a big help today." Ava scrawled on the pad. She put the pad back in the drawer, closed it, and placed the pen back on the desk. "Well, I better get back to my station."

Catt walked to her desk and opened the drawer. Nothing appeared out of place. Was Ava really looking for a Post-it or was she just being her nosy self?

Catt grabbed the pad. Ava's writing had indented the next sticky note. Catt viewed the Post-it. She could not make out what she wrote. She moved closer to the bay window for more light. The words "Don't forget" appeared on the pad. Don't forget what? Catt put the pad back in the drawer. She used the restroom and headed back to the fair to check on the food station.

The volunteers were busy handing food to the guests while Beau and Jonathan Ray replenished the items.

Catt stepped behind the tables to help during the lunchtime rush.

"We need more paper plates and cups," a volunteer said to Catt.

"I'll get them. I have extras in the shed." Catt grabbed the rope key behind the grill and unlocked the shed door. As she tried to open the door, something heavy pressed against it from the other side. She pushed again but was not able to open it. Beau and a volunteer came up behind her. "Did you get the plates and cups?" Beau asked.

"I can't get the door to open."

"Here. Let me help." Beau shoved the door, but it wouldn't budge. He used his shoulder to push harder. Finally, it slid open. Beau stepped inside the shed. Catt and the volunteer followed.

The volunteer put her hands to her face and screamed. "Oh...no."

A crowd gathered.

"He's dead," someone yelled.

Catt knelt by Richard's body. Pruner shears protruded from his back. She checked his pulse and shook her head. Flashbacks of finding two of her clients murdered in the past raced through her mind.

A tear escaped the corner of her eye.

CHAPTER EIGHT

After the medical examiner removed the body, Detective Monroe questioned guests about Richard. Who saw him? Was there anything suspicious during the event? It made Catt's head spin. She sat at a picnic table with all her helpers. The rest of the guests cleared out. The dogs played in the yard among the other police officers and crime scene tape as if nothing had happened.

Vanessa placed her hands on the table, stood, and then leaned forward. "If you ask me, someone didn't want him around for a reason."

"Well, that's obvious," Beau said.

"But who?" Em asked.

"I was standing by the medical examiner when they removed him from the shed. He suspects that Richard had been dead for about twelve hours," Ava remarked.

"Catt, didn't you say that you and Beau had some beers with Richard last night and he walked to his house around ten-thirty?" Jonathan Ray asked.

"That's right. He said he was tired and would see us this morning. But I never saw him again."

"Exactly. Then you and Beau were the last to see him. And based on that information, it means one or both of you did him in and hid him in the shed," Vanessa suggested.

"Are you crazy? Why would we do that?" Catt crossed her arms.

"Well, I heard that Beau here is a convict, and you and Richard did not get along. That's two motives for murder. You probably put the supplies in my yard to draw attention toward me," Vanessa suggested.

Detective Monroe stood behind the group and cleared his throat. Catt had not realized he was standing there. "While I appreciate everyone being Sherlock Holmes, let's leave the detective work to me." He turned toward Catt and Em. "I need to talk to you both privately for a few minutes."

Catt and Em rose from the table.

"Okay. So, here's the deal." He pulled a notepad and pen from his pocket. "First we have a theft of stolen items from your shed. Then according to my interview with Vanessa Carlson earlier, the items were found in her front yard. Is there a reason you didn't tell me they were found?" He pointed his pen toward Catt.

"No. I mean, yes. I was in the middle of doing last minute tasks for today. I was running out of time getting things ready."

The detective raised his eyebrows. "I see. Ms. Carlson said that your handyman and Richard picked up the items from her yard and brought them back here."

Catt nodded.

"Then what happened to everything?"

"Beau and I put them in the shed."

The detective frowned. "Well that would mean you went into the shed first thing this morning to pull them out for today's event."

"Actually, Beau had them set up when I walked into the backyard this morning."

"Did he have a key?"

"Yes. I told him where I hid it."

"Then he would have had to see Richard's body, since the medical examiner estimated he died at least twelve hours earlier."

"Beau didn't mention it."

The detective called Beau over and questioned him about the timeline of events.

"When I arrived this morning, the supplies and bottled water were sitting outside the shed, so I put them on the tables. I assumed that Catt had put them out for me."

"And why is that?"

"The night before, we talked about that being one of my first tasks this morning."

"Did you put the supplies outside the shed for Beau?" the detective asked Catt.

"No. They were in the shed where we left them yesterday."

"You didn't think it was odd they were outside?" he asked Beau.

"Not really."

"Did you notice anything suspicious?"

"No," Beau said.

"So, no one had to go into the shed until lunch today?" he asked Catt.

Catt's face was blank. She did not understand how this could happen. "I guess not. I didn't go in there until we needed to replenish items during lunch."

"Any idea how Richard ended up dead in your shed?"

Catt, Em, and Beau shook their heads. Ava, James, Jonathan Ray, Brock, Vanessa, Sammy, and Rhea gathered around them.

"I understand from the group chat at the picnic table, that you two had beers with Richard last night?" he asked Catt and Beau.

"That's correct," Catt said.

"What happened next?"

"Richard walked home around ten thirty and said he would see us this morning to help set up. But I never saw him again until we found him." Catt rubbed her forehead. The stress of it all was getting to her. She paused. "But we did hear something in the bushes at Richard's a short while after he went home."

"And what was it?" the detective asked.

"Beau checked but didn't see anything. We assumed it was a cat that roams the neighborhood."

"Interesting." The detective made a note in his notepad.

"Something else," Catt said. "Vanessa went to Richard's house this morning, knocked on the door but no one answered."

"Ms. Carlson mentioned that during my interview with her."

Vanessa frowned at Catt.

"What time did the two of you call it a night?" the detective asked Catt.

Catt glanced at Beau. "Around midnight."

"That sounds right," Beau said.

Em stood silent looking at her sister.

"What were you two doing between ten thirty and twelve last night?"

"Talking," Catt said.

Beau nodded.

"You didn't see or hear anyone else besides the cat?"

"Now that I think of it there was one thing, after Beau left. I heard what sounded like two gunshots. My dogs were barking like crazy but I shrugged it off as fireworks."

"What time was that?"

"Around twelve thirty maybe."

The detective made a note. "One last item. The original key that was missing from the rope. Was that ever found?"

"No," Catt said.

"I need you two not to leave Virginia Beach during the investigation," Detective Monroe said to Catt and Beau. "But that's all for now. I'll be in touch."

CHAPTER NINE

After a restless night, Catt texted Sammy and Em to cover the day's schedule. She was not in the right frame of mind to walk the dogs, and she needed to finish cleaning up the yard from the fair. They responded the schedule was covered. Catt turned on the TV and jumped on the treadmill in her bedroom to burn off stress. Cagney and Lacey rested in their beds quietly. It was as if they knew something was wrong with Catt.

The news anchor reported the murder of Richard Boykins. The anchor stated that Richard was found dead with pruning shears in his back, in the shed of sisters Catt and Em Ramsey, with Catt being the last to see him the night before.

"They think I murdered him." Catt stopped the treadmill and raised her voice. "What the hell?"

Her phone rang.

"Did you see the news?" Em asked.

"They think I did it."

"That's all we need is to be accused of another murder. I have to ask, did Beau have anything to do with it?"

Catt frowned. "I just don't know what to think at this point."

"What about Vanessa? She was at Richard's the next morning."

"Maybe it's a diversion to give her an alibi if someone saw her at his house last night if she murdered him," Catt suggested.

"But how would she have gotten him into the shed? She is tiny, and Richard was stout."

161

"True. Where did the pruning shears come from?" Catt asked.

"I'm thinking they belonged to Richard," Em offered.

"That makes sense. He was always out there pruning his roses."

"After I walk the dogs, I'll view the footage to see who was in the bushes that you and Beau heard."

"Wait, Em. Before you hang up, tell me what you found out from the other footage?"

"Not much. It showed the front and side of my house and down the driveway but not the shed. But I sent it to Detective Monroe anyway. Once I view last night's video, I'll send him that one too. Oh...Jonathan Ray will be installing new cameras on the property."

"That's good. We need them. I'll question Beau to feel him out a little more and Vanessa to find out why she went to Richard's. And something else worth checking out, Catt said.

"What?"

"I caught Ava nosing in my office desk drawer during the fair."

"What?"

"Said she was looking for a Post-it to make herself a reminder. I told her to grab it from the drawer. After she left, I looked at the indented writing on the note below it. It had 'don't forget.'"

"What does that mean?"

"I have no clue."

"She kept calling me to relieve her during the fair. I thought she had problems. Let's keep our eyes and ears open. Gotta go."

After Catt finished her twenty-minute workout on the treadmill, she sat on the floor and played with Cagney and Lacey. They nudged their noses to give her kisses and wagged their tails affectionately. She walked to her office and put on a pot of coffee. It was ready by the time she finished showering. She was glad that Sammy and Em had the schedule covered today.

While sipping her first cup of the day, she strolled to the bay window in her office. Beau was taking down the rails from

Pawject Runway. She finished her coffee and headed down the stairs, with the dogs trailing behind.

"Good morning, beautiful." Beau broke the runway rails down, and then placed each piece on the ground.

"You need help with that?" Catt asked.

"Sure. Take these and place them in the bed of my truck." He nodded toward where it was parked at the end of the driveway.

As Catt grabbed the rails and put them in the bed, the portable toilet company entered the driveway.

Beau greeted the driver to handle the pickup.

Catt continued to grab the items until she had all of them loaded in the truck.

After the company left, Catt approached Beau. "Thanks for handling that."

"You got it. You ready to put the tables in the shed?" Beau asked.

"Sure." Catt was glad that Beau was taking the lead. She grabbed the key and unlocked the shed. It was difficult entering the building after finding Richard. But she and Beau had cleaned up the blood stains and mess earlier. She stepped to the side as Beau leaned the tables against the shelf. Her stomach rumbled, reminding her that it was almost lunchtime.

He wiped his face with his shirt sleeve and chugged a bottle of water. They exited the shed, and Catt locked the door.

"So, do you have any thoughts about Richard's murder?"

"Like what?" Beau asked.

Catt shrugged. "Like, who did it?"

Before he could respond, the dogs started barking. Vanessa approached from the driveway with Pookie. "Hi, there," she said.

"What are you and Pookie up to?" Catt asked.

"Just taking a walk to clear my head. I can't stop thinking about Richard. We'd been moving toward a more serious relationship. I can't believe he is gone."

"I understand." Catt's instinct told her not to trust Vanessa's motive for stopping by.

Beau headed to the truck and shut the truck gate. "I'll run

these back to the supplier since he's only open for a short time today. I'm grabbing lunch while I'm out. Can I get you something?"

"No, thanks. I have plenty to eat," Catt said.

"Nothing for me. Pookie and I are heading home."

"Okay. I'll finish the rest of the clean up when I get back." Beau drove off.

Vanessa turned toward Richard's house. "His house looks sad without him there."

Catt faced Vanessa. "Tell me. Why *did* you go to Richard's house yesterday morning?"

"To see if he wanted to attend the fair together."

"You mentioned the dogs were barking. Did you see anyone during that time?"

"Listen. As much as I would love to answer your questions I have to go. Catch you later." Vanessa walked Pookie down the driveway and into the street.

Catt scratched her head. She had a lot to think about.

CHAPTER TEN

The next day, Catt sat at her desk modifying the schedule due to cancellations from several clients. Although nobody came right out and said it, word on the street was they did not want their dogs walked by someone involved in a murder investigation.

Catt received texts from both Rhea and Brock to walk Pritzie and Grayson. She added them to the schedule and was grateful for their business.

The door swung open, and Em entered. "Check this out." She held out her cell phone. "Now that Jonathan Ray has all the cameras on the property, I can see everything."

Catt viewed the phone screen as Em scrolled through different views of the property. "Wow. I'm glad he got it working. Can you add the app to my phone?"

"Sure."

Catt handed Em her phone.

"Did you find anything helpful on the old surveillance system?" Catt asked.

"Here's the thing. There was someone standing in Richard's bushes the night that you and Beau heard something."

"Who was it?"

"I couldn't tell. The old system was so antiquated, it was impossible to make out who it was. But get this. The person had a svelte shape," Em said.

Catt's eyebrows knitted together. "Interesting. Before Richard died, he said his cameras showed a small figure."

"I think it was a woman's silhouette. Vanessa has a sexy,

hour-glass shape," Em added.

"Well, get this. She came by here yesterday."

"What did she want?"

"Said she was walking Pookie and missing Richard."

"Do you think she's spying on his house and us? I mean if that was her that you and Beau heard that night that's pretty suspicious."

"Right. The guilty person coming back to the crime scene." I don't know what to make of everything," Catt said.

Em handed Catt her phone. "All done. Click on the app to scroll through the pages."

Catt viewed live images on her phone. "This is awesome. Thanks."

"I wish we had it before."

The door swung open. "Knock. Knock." Detective Monroe entered. "Good morning. Have a few minutes for some questions?"

"Uh...sure. Have a seat." Catt waved her hand toward a chair in front of her desk.

"I'm glad you're both here. Since Richard's daughter gave us permission to check the cameras on his property, we could see a figure in the bushes but couldn't tell who it was."

"Richard has a daughter?" Catt asked.

"Yes. You didn't know that?" Detective Monroe asked.

"No. We've never been very close."

"I have something," Em said. "I looked at my surveillance again and the night that Catt and Beau heard someone in the bushes, the video showed a figure that appeared to be a woman. But I can't make out who it is."

"Did you send me that?" The detective asked.

"Yes."

"There are new cameras on the property," the detective pointed out.

"Yes, since the murder, we beefed up our security."

The detective viewed his notes. "We determined one gunshot wound killed Richard."

"Richard didn't die from the pruning shears?" Catt asked.

"That came later. Apparently, the shears covered up the gunshot wound when you found him. So, whoever did it really wanted him dead. But we also found Richard's prints on the shears, which had his initials on them, written with a Sharpie."

"So, they belonged to Richard?" Catt asked.

"Yes." The detective flipped through his notes. "Regarding the night that you and Beau were talking on the veranda. You said you went to bed around midnight."

"Yes."

"As mentioned previously, the medical examiner determined the time of death around midnight. But you said you heard two gunshots around twelve thirty?"

"That's correct. Do you think one of them was the shot that killed him?" Catt said.

"The timeline fits." Detective Monroe made a note on his pad. "That's all the questions I have for now."

"Am I a suspect?" Catt asked.

He closed his pad. "Look. My job is to cover all bases. I'll be in touch." He headed out the door and down the stairs.

Catt trembled. Was he going to arrest her?

Em took her hand. "It will be okay. We've been through this before. Do you want me to walk Pritzie and Grayson?"

"I appreciate it, sis, but it will be good for me to walk them."

CHAPTER ELEVEN

Catt headed to Rhea's apartment to pick up Pritzie. When she unlocked the door, Pritzie came running down the hallway in another cute pink outfit, barking. "Hey, girl. Where's your leash?" Pritzie ran into the kitchen, and Catt followed.

Rhea entered from the living room. She was dressed in a pink workout outfit and holding a photo album. "Hi, Catt."

"Rhea. I thought you were out."

"Oh…I'm running behind. I got caught up in looking through old photos. But I'm heading to the gym for my morning workout." She set the album on the table.

Catt grabbed Pritzie's leash from the table, and then turned and faced Rhea. Catt had not realized it before, but Rhea was slim. Her tight workout clothes revealed bulging muscles. "You look great."

"Oh, thanks. I've been lifting weights, jumping on the treadmill, and doing other exercises." Rhea gave Pritzie a kiss. "Catt, how are you doing?"

"I've been better."

"I caught the news. Do they have a suspect?"

"Besides me?"

"It was such a terrible end to the fair. Did the police figure out why he was in your shed?"

"That's the million-dollar question."

"Were there any witnesses?" Rhea petted Pritzie.

"No."

"That's too bad. Did he have any family?"

"There's a daughter. She lives out of state but traveled to Virginia to handle the funeral arrangements and estate details."

"Oh good. Well…you can just leave Pritzie in the apartment when you're done. Oh…I almost forgot. Ava mentioned at the fair that she saw you on the boardwalk the other day walking Pritzie and Grayson. Remember that I asked you not to walk Pritzie with other dogs?" Rhea said.

Why would Ava tell Rhea? "I'm sorry. It was to save time." Some of Catt's clients refused to recognize that it helped her save time and money to walk the dogs together.

"It's okay since Brock and I are back together. So, you can walk her with Grayson. Afterall, they're practically brother and sister now. Too-da-loo."

Oh, brother.

Rhea headed out the door.

Catt found it strange that Rhea and Brock were back together. But if they were happy who was she to disapprove?

The dog was so excited to walk that she knocked the album off the table. Catt leaned down and gathered the photos off the floor. One photo showed a young Rhea with a man next to her, his arm around her tiny waist. He seemed familiar. Catt turned the photo over but there was nothing on the back. On a hunch, she pulled out her phone and took a picture of the front of the photo. She put the photos back in the album and set it on the table. She and Pritzie headed down the hall to Brock's apartment.

Grayson stood on his hind legs as Catt opened the door. Pritzie ran ahead to greet her friend. "Hi Grayson." Brock was out for the day, so Catt leashed Grayson and off the three went to the boardwalk.

CHAPTER TWELVE

It had been four days since Richard's murder, and the press was still reporting that Catt was a suspect. More clients canceled their appointments.

Last night, Catt and Em had delivered food to Richard's daughter to pay their respect as neighbors. When talking to her, they discovered she had not seen him in years due to his hard drinking. Catt assured her that she had nothing to do with her father's death.

Although his daughter was grateful for the food, she came right out and said she did not know what to believe about her father's murder.

Catt, Em, and Jonathan Ray attended Richard's funeral together. Vanessa, Rhea, Brock, Beau, Ava and James were all in attendance, too. That surprised Catt, but she assumed it was to pay their respects, since they were there when his body was discovered.

After the funeral, Catt headed home and entered her bedroom. She changed from her funeral clothes to shorts and a Woof-Pack t-shirt. Sammy and Em were out walking dogs of the few clients who remained. The murder weighed heavy on her mind. Not only was she under suspicion, but she needed to clear her name.

The door swung open, and Beau entered the office.

Catt walked down the narrow hallway from her bedroom to the front office.

"How's it going?" he asked.

She sat down at her desk. "Uh…it's been an emotional, few days." Catt placed her hands on her face. "And my business is taking a hit because of all the negative publicity."

"I know this is hard on you. Do the police have any leads?"

"Not yet. But I keep racking my brain about the thefts and how Richard ended up in my shed. I can't figure any of it out."

Beau moved closer to Catt. "Here. Let me help." He rubbed her shoulders. "You are stressed."

Catt took a deep breath as he relieved the tension.

Em entered the office. Her eyes widened at Beau rubbing Catt's shoulders.

Beau removed his hands from Catt. "Well…I'm heading out for the day. I finished cutting the grass and did the chores. See you tomorrow." He headed down the stairs.

"What the hell was he doing?" Em placed her hands on her hips.

Catt rolled her eyes. "He was trying to relieve my stress."

"Look. I know it's none of my business but it's not very smart to have a fling with an employee, especially an ex con."

Catt frowned. "You're right. It's none of your business." Catt changed the subject. "I have an update on the case."

"Oh?"

"When I went to Rheas' a few days ago, there was something odd."

"Like what?"

"A photo album was on the kitchen table. When I leashed Pritzie, she was so excited she knocked it off the table. I looked at the pictures that fell out. One was odd."

"What was it?"

"A picture of Rhea standing with a man when she was younger." Catt grabbed her phone and scrolled through her photos. "Look at this." She held out her phone for Em to see.

"I recognize Rhea. But who's that with her?"

"Doesn't it look like Richard?"

"No. Are you crazy? I think this is getting to you."

Catt turned the phone back toward herself. She viewed the photo. "You're right. I'm looking for clues that aren't there." Catt ran her hand through her long blond hair.

"It's okay. Detective Monroe will figure it all out."

"I hope it's soon."

"The other thing to figure out is Beau. Today's massage tells me this isn't the first time he's given you relief."

"Em. Don't make more out of it than it is."

"Good. Because we still don't know if Beau is involved."

CHAPTER THIRTEEN

Catt sat at her desk the next day making a few notations on a notepad about things that may, or may not, have a bearing on Richard's murder. Why would someone steal her supplies and put them in Vanessa's yard? Vanessa knocking on Richard's door the morning after his death had been out of the ordinary, but why? Was it to cover her tracks if someone had seen her the night before in the bushes? The gunshots? Beau's criminal history for robbery? The supplies outside the shed on Saturday morning? Wasn't that suspicious? Had Beau moved them? Ava searching through Catt's desk, what was that about? Rhea's photo that resembled Richard? So many questions, so few answers.

Cagney, Lacey, and Grayson wanted to go outside to play. Catt was keeping Grayson for the day while Brock attended an event. He would pick him up later.

She opened the door and let them outside. They raced down the steps. She went back inside to finish writing down her thoughts.

Em and Sammy entered the office after finishing their walks for the day. They checked on Catt, grabbed a few treats and headed outside to play with the dogs. Catt stayed behind, wanting more time alone with her thoughts.

The door swung open. Rhea entered. "How's it going, Catt?"

Startled, Catt turned toward Rhea. "What are you doing here?"

Rhea held Pritzie in her arms.

"I was walking Pritzie and thought that Grayson might need

175

a playmate."

"How did you know he was here?"

"Brock told me."

Catt noticed Pritzie was panting. "Does Pritzie need some water?"

"Sure." Rhea set Pritzie on the floor.

Catt reached into the mini fridge. "Shoot. I'm out of water. Be right back. I have to go to the supply closet."

Catt returned from grabbing water to find Rhea standing near her desk. Her hand rested on her notepad.

Catt frowned. "Here's some water for Pritzie." She grabbed a bowl, filled it and tossed the bottle in the recycle bin.

Pritzie walked to the bowl for a drink.

Catt unhooked Pritzie's leash and set it on her desk.

"So. You're out with Pritzie today?"

"Yeah. But my thoughts are with you."

"Oh. Why me?"

"Well. I was kicking around the day you were in my apartment to walk Pritzie. When I returned from the gym, the photos in the album were out of order. That's when I was thinking you had looked at them."

"Uh…sorry about that. Pritzie knocked the book off the table, and they fell out."

"I see. There was one photo that was on top. A photo of me and a man with his arm around my waist. Do you recall that photo?"

"No," Catt lied. "Why?"

Pritzie finished drinking the water and made her way to a doggie bed, where she curled up and settled down for a nap.

"After I picked up Pritzie at your house about a month ago when you watched her, Richard recognized me as I walked down the stairs. He called my name. A name I haven't used in years. A name associated with my former life before I became Rhea Lucas Prentiss."

Catt tilted her head.

Rhea walked closer toward Catt. She ran her fingers around the corner of the desk then down the notepad. "I knew you had recognized Richard in the photo. You even noted it here." She pointed toward the notepad.

"I don't understand."

"When Richard recognized me and found out I was living in the loft, he realized I had money. And he wanted it."

"Are you saying he was blackmailing you?"

"That's exactly what I'm saying. When we were young, Richard and I were involved in illegal activity. We ran scams throughout Virginia. A kind of Bonnie and Clyde."

"What type of scams?"

"We would go into neighborhoods, sell fake magazine subscriptions for a charitable cause for cash only. Only, we'd pocket the cash. Made a killing."

"But Richard seemed so against that type of behavior."

"Now he is. Or was. I should say. But he's been struggling to pay bills and demanded money from me. So, I gave him five thousand dollars. Then he asked for more. That's when I realized it was the beginning and would never end."

"Why are you telling me all of this?"

Rhea smiled. "Why do you think?"

Catt bit her lip. "You killed Richard?"

"You got it."

"But how?"

"When I found out you were having an event, I knew it was the perfect time to sneak into Richard's house, shoot him, and drag him to your shed. I needed someone to take the rap. You were perfect since you lived next door. And I had remembered you saying in the past that you had issues with your neighbor. But what I didn't expect was you and lover boy Beau to be out on the veranda that night.

"That was you in the bushes?" Her gaze darted around the room, looking for an escape route.

"Yes."

"Why did you stab him after you shot him? He was already dead?"

"That was for extra measure."

"How did you get in the shed?"

"I took the key off the rope that hung on the shed. Tsk, tsk. Leaving a key outside is like inviting someone to rob you."

"So, you took the key and put the supplies and water outside?"

"Yes. I wanted to put Richard on a shelf, to display him, so to say. I pulled everything out to make room, but he had gained so much weight, I could only drag him, not lift him."

Catt could not understand any of this. "Did you also steal the supplies and water?"

"Of course. I needed to make room in the shed. When I stopped by to make another payment to Richard, I waited until you left your property, took the stuff out and put them on Vanessa's property hoping you'd blame her. Richard had left to deposit the money so I knew he wouldn't see me."

"You know Vanessa?"

"See. Vanessa and I go way back with Richard. She was the reason he and I broke up years ago. And now that you know the truth, I have to kill you too."

Rhea moved closer. She pulled a rope from her pocket and leaned forward.

Before Catt could duck or run, Rhea wrapped the rope around Catt's neck and pulled it tight.

Catt grabbed the rope trying to free herself, but the rope tightened. The pressure on her neck made it difficult to breathe. She tried to scream, but no sounds came out. Her fingers fumbled against the hard fibers of the rope. She looked at Rhea's face. The look of determination on her face bordered on maniacal.

Catt didn't want to die. Panic rose in her belly as her tongue swelled and her eyes started bugging from their sockets. She somehow found the strength to kick Rhea several times.

"Ow, that hurt." Rhea loosened her grip.

Catt's gaze swept the room, looking for a weapon. Something. Anything. Pritzie's leash on her desk was her only choice. Reaching, stretching, her hand snaked toward the leash. She grabbed it tight between her fingers then raised it high above her head. Adrenaline kicked in, and with every ounce of energy she possessed in her body, she swung the leash against Rhea's face.

Rhea fell back, dropping the rope.

Catt made her move toward the door.

Rhea grabbed Catt's foot and yanked her to the ground.

Catt fell, smacking her head against the wooden floor. She screamed for help, hoping Em and Sammy would hear.

Pritzie barked.

Rhea sat on top of Catt and placed the rope around her neck again.

Catt bit Rhea's hand, hanging on like a dog with a bone.

"Ouch. You, bitch!"

Catt coughed and choked but was able to take advantage of her distraction to wrangle herself from under Rhea.

The door swung open. Em and Sammy rushed in, with Cagney, Lacey, and Grayson. Dogs to the rescue!

Rhea stood and rushed toward the door.

"Stop her," Catt yelled. "She admitted to killing Richard, and she tried to kill me." Catt coughed and rubbed her neck.

Em grabbed the leash and swung the metal part against Rhea's head. She fell across the doorway. Cagney and Lacey got tangled around her ankles, and Rhea fell hard to the landing.

Catt scrambled up and gave chase, not wanting the killer to get away.

Rhea kicked the dogs away and raised to her feet.

Beau stood at the bottom of the stairs. "What the hell?"

Em ran out the door and swung the leash at Rhea again.

Rhea ducked and raced down the steps.

"Stop her," Em screamed. "She tried to kill Catt."

Rhea leapt down the final steps and barreled into Beau.

Beau wrapped his arms around Rhea's waist and dragged her to the ground. The two wrestled in the grass. Beau managed to get the upper hand. With Rhea face down on the ground, Beau pushed his knee into Rhea's back and held her down.

"Call 9-1-1," Em yelled.

Sammy used her cellphone to report the emergency.

The dogs circled around Rhea barking and snapping. Pritzie

stood next to her mom, not understanding what was happening.

Jonathan Ray pulled into the driveway. He paused for a moment, taking the scene in, before jumping out of the car and racing over. He helped Beau hold Rhea.

Em walked over to Catt and placed a comforting arm around her.

Brock walked into the backyard to pick up Grayson. "What in the world is going on?"

Detective Monroe rushed into the yard and stopped short.

"What are you doing here?" Catt asked the detective.

"We enhanced the video that Em sent me. Rhea murdered Richard."

"Tell us something we don't already know," Catt said.

They all laughed. All except Rhea, that is.

Two hours later, Catt walked into the backyard, holding a tray of snacks, beer, and wine. "I think we need this." She offered the tray to Sammy, who grabbed a glass of wine.

Nosy Ava and James came right over. "We heard about the arrest! I never would have figured Rhea to be a killer!"

"I know," Catt said. "Me either. We're celebrating her arrest. Who else wants a drink?" Catt asked.

"I'll take the chilled Rosé," Em said.

"A cold one for me," Brock said.

"White wine please." Ava smiled.

"Same for me," Vanessa said.

"Beer for me," James said.

Detective Monroe grabbed a beer from the tray. "Off duty now." He smiled.

Catt set the tray on a table and poured herself a glass of wine. She took the chair next to Brock. "How are you feeling since Rhea's arrest?"

"It's a lot to take in. But there were villainous signs. It worked out for the best." Brock clinked glasses with Catt. She rose and walked over to be next to Beau who sat by the detective. "What will happen to Rhea?" she asked the detective.

"Now that we have her confession, she'll sit in jail until a hearing and sentencing are set." He paused, watching the dogs play in the yard. "Will someone foster Pritzie?"

"Yes. I recommended someone to the authorities," Catt said.

"Is Richard's daughter taking his dogs?" Vanessa asked.

"Yes," Catt sipped her wine.

"I hope Rhea goes to prison for a long time," Ava said.

"Me, too." Em clinked glasses with Ava.

Catt was glad to see Em and Ava bonding.

Catt leaned toward Ava since she was fanning herself. "You okay?"

"I'm having my own personal summer. She lowered her voice. I'm going through menopause. Can I sit in your office in front of the AC for a few minutes like I did during the doggie fair? It was a lifesaver that day."

Catt smiled since that answered her question about why Ava kept going to her office. "Sure. Stay as long as you like."

Jonathan Ray grabbed a beer and popped the top. "While we're sharing good news, Em and I are taking a metal detecting trip to the Eastern Shore since the case is now solved."

Catt raised her glass toward Em.

"Hear, hear!" the group said in unison.

Catt turned toward Beau. "By the way, are you staying on as my handyman?"

Beau sipped his beer. "Of course. Why?"

"Two reasons. First, I am promoting you to maintenance supervisor since you showed great leadership during the fair and murder investigation."

"And the other reason?"

"Let's just say I'm looking at it." She winked at Beau. "Cheers."

THE END

STRUT YOUR MUTT
By Heather Weidner

Sassy Private Investigator, Delanie Fitzgerald, plans to spend her day off relaxing at the mall's Strut Your Mutt festival, where her partner's English bulldog is a finalist in a pampered doggie pageant. Little did she know that Margaret the bulldog would turn into an overnight social media influencer and a magnet for new clients. The phone starts ringing with a distraught woman who needs help finding a missing dog. But this French poodle is no ordinary pooch. This star of the dog show circuit has been dognapped. Delanie, and her computer hacker partner, Duncan Reynolds, sniff out information from the deep web and put paws to the pavement to track down clues to the dog's whereabouts.

Delanie gets more than she bargains for when she wrestles a suspect, chases down leads at dog shelters, and uncovers a body. But can she find the missing poodle before it's too late?

HEATHER WEIDNER is the author of the three Delanie Fitzgerald Mystery novels and these characters appear in this novella, "Strut Your Mutt." Her short stories appear in the Virginia is for Mysteries *series,* 50 Shades of Cabernet, *and* Deadly Southern Charm. *Her dog-themed novellas appear in the Mutt Mysteries series, and her new Jules Keene Glamping mysteries is slated for release in October 2021.*

Heather lives in Central Virginia with her husband and a pair of Jack Russell terriers. She earned her BA in English from Virginia Wesleyan University and her MA in American literature from the University of Richmond. Through the years, she has been a cop's kid, technical writer, editor, college professor, software tester, and IT manager.

Website and Blog: http://www.heatherweidner.com

CHAPTER ONE

Hundreds of dogs covered almost every inch of outdoor space at the Stony Point Fashion Park. Delanie Fitzgerald waded through a sea of dogs and humans to the large stage in the plaza area. She looked around for her partner, Duncan Reynolds. Not seeing anyone who resembled the computer geek who was the other half of the Falcon Investigations team, she stood on a low stone wall for a better view.

"Hey, there you are."

She hopped down and turned to face Duncan and his sidekick, Margaret, a brown and white English bulldog. In the office, Margaret had two speeds, slow and napping. Today, she seemed more interested in all the other dogs.

"I'm glad you could come to support us," he said.

"Of course. You and Margaret are like family." Delanie scanned the crowd of people, many in elaborate costumes that matched their dogs. Delanie's favorites were the superheroes and their sidekicks.

"We've got to get ready. Right after the Strut Your Mutt fashion show, Pickles will be signing autographs."

Delanie furrowed her brow. "Pickles?"

"I sent you the link to the video. Pickles the Pug. She and her handler are social media influencers. She's got a bazillion followers."

"The dog's a social media influencer?" Delanie looked at Margaret and then at the dogs who were milling around the plaza area.

"Yup. She built her following with funny memes and videos, and now she does appearances and product endorsements. Pickles is today's headliner for Pooch-a-palooza. Evie's here, too. She's going to video Margaret's fashion debut. And then she'll grab us a spot in line. Margaret wants to meet Pickles."

Delanie smiled. Evie Hachey was Duncan's steady girlfriend. They had met a few summers ago at a comicon, and she was the perfect complement to her geeky partner, who did web design when he wasn't getting computers to cough up information from the seedy corners of the Dark Web for the firm's investigations.

"Make sure to get a good spot and lots of pictures. I'm going to set up an Instagram account and a webpage for Margaret tonight. The Adventures of Margaret the Wonder Dog." He glanced down at his Apple Watch that looked like something out of the Dick Tracy comics. "We've got to get on stage." Duncan shifted a large black backpack to his other shoulder and guided Margaret through the crowd.

The crowd, already five and six people deep, continued to grow. Delanie strolled toward the stage and found a spot near the large fountain.

Ten minutes later, the local weatherman, Zac Parker, and a woman walked up to the edge of the stage. "Hello, RVA," he said. "Welcome to the first Pooch-a-palooza. Hey, you Richmond folks, you're in for a treat today. Are you excited?"

The crowd roared, and dogs started barking.

"We'll be starting the Strut Your Mutt fashion show in a few minutes. At two o'clock, Pickles the Pug will be here at the stage in front of the bookstore. She'll be signing books and calendars. You won't want to miss her. And then it will be time for everyone to get in on the act for the Furry Scurry of Paws on Parade at three o'clock. And Yappy Hour starts at all the restaurants and pubs here at four. Check out the drink and snack specials. So, who's ready for some fun?"

The dogs and their human friends let out whoops, barks, and howls of appreciation.

"Okay then," Zac said. "Before we start the show, I'd like to introduce Dee Caruthers. She's the Director of the Central

Virginia Animal League."

The tall woman with a blunt-cut bob strode across the stage. "Thank you, Zac. I'd like to thank all of you and your gorgeous pets for coming out today to support our furry friends. Today's proceeds are going to the CVAL, and we are so appreciative of your generosity. And if you'd like to know more about our organization, stop by the purple tent by the food court. Our folks would love to talk to you about adoption, fostering, or volunteering."

"Thanks, Dee. People, go over and check them out. So, without further ado, I'd like to introduce the contestants for Strut Your Mutt. This year, CVAL had an online fundraiser to see which pet and his human could raise the most money. Today, we feature the top five, and you'll have a chance to vote in a few minutes for your favorite. I just want to say that these five pairs raised over seven thousand dollars for CVAL. Isn't that amazing?"

When the cheering subsided, Zac continued, "Okay, let's meet these fabulous animals. First, we have Dixie and her friend, Pam. Dixie is a teacup chihuahua who likes to snuggle and read romance novels." The tiny white dog danced onto the stage in a red bodysuit and tutu that matched what her owner was wearing. "Next, we have Bruno and his friend, Jackson. Bruno is a harlequin Great Dane who likes car rides and swimming in the pool." The dog, the size of a small pony, dragged his owner to the front of the stage. Bruno sported a faux leather jacket and a pair of mirrored shades.

"Next, we have Margaret and her friend, Duncan. Margaret is an English bulldog who goes to work every day at Falcon Investigations as a private eye. Today, she's sporting her Sherlock Bones costume." Margaret waddled across the stage and plopped down near the edge. Duncan followed in his trench coat and pipe, a perfect Dr. Watson sidekick. Delanie put two fingers in her mouth and let out an ear-piercing whistle for the pair.

Zac stepped back. "Now, let's meet Jeff and his friend, Robert. Jeff's a basset hound who loves tummy rubs, treats, and baseball." The chubby dog lumbered out on the stage with a

Washington Nats hat and jersey.

"And last, but certainly not least, is Hobbes, the golden doodle, who is here with his pal, Jayden. When he's not working as a comfort dog, Hobbes enjoys long walks and naps. He hangs out most days with his best friend, Calvin the cat." The golden doodle, groomed like a lion, danced on stage and greeted all the other dogs.

"And those are your five contestants. No matter what the outcome of today's voting, I think you're all winners. Okay, so let's circle the stage with your pets twice, so everyone can get a good look, and then we'll line up across the front."

"Who Let the Dogs Out" blared on the speakers as the dogs and their owners paraded around the stage. The fans cheered and waved.

Zac tapped on his microphone several times. The thunking sounds echoed across the plaza. "Okay, folks. You've seen them all. You ready to vote?" When the crowd noise subsided, he continued, "I'm going to step behind each contestant, and you're going to vote with your applause. Dee is going to help me determine who got the most crowd support. Ready? Let's start with Dixie."

The crowd cheered for Dixie and Bruno. Then it was Margaret's turn. Delanie yelled and hooted as loud as she could. Margaret looked around and then plopped down on the stage. The crowd laughed and continued to cheer. Zac moved on to Jeff and Hobbes. When the applause died down, Zac and Dee put their heads together to confer.

"That was close. Let me have Dixie and Margaret come to the front of the stage. We're going to do a runoff between the two ladies." This time, Margaret danced around Duncan's legs and woofed along with the crowd.

Dee leaned forward to whisper to Zac.

"I think we have a winner," he said. "This year's Pooch-a-palooza Strut Your Mutt Winner is Margaret as Sherlock Bones. You've won a one-hundred-dollar gift certificate, a gift basket from our sponsors, and an interview tomorrow with me on Channel 6."

"Thanks, so much," Duncan said. "Margaret and I are so excited." Right on cue, the pudgy, brown and white log with legs slid to a resting position. Only her eyes moved as she watched the crowd.

Zac laughed as someone handed Duncan a huge basket and an envelope. "Folks, Pickles the Pug will be at a table in front of the bookstore in ten minutes. Make sure you stop by and pick up some great pug gear. Thanks again." They disappeared off stage.

Delanie spotted Duncan and Margaret standing with three photographers at the base of the stage. Margaret didn't seem too excited about her big win. She lay down and yawned.

When the crowds moved on and everyone had congratulated Duncan and Margaret, Delanie moved closer. "This is awesome." She leaned down and hugged Margaret. "Do you want me to carry the basket?"

"Nah," Duncan said. "I'm going to put this stuff in the car. Do you mind staying with Margaret for a minute? I need to find Evie. I'll meet you over at the line to see Pickles."

Delanie and Margaret wended their way through the crowds. The line snaked around the front of the bookstore and down a row of shops. She hadn't realized how popular the little pug was. While they waited in line, Delanie scanned Facebook and Instagram and checked out photos of Pickles.

As Delanie started getting restless from standing, Duncan and Evie appeared. "Thanks for holding a place for us. It looks like Margaret's beat from all the excitement." Margaret lay sprawled on the pavement.

"Hi, Evie. It's good to see you again," Delanie said.

The smallish woman behind the tortoise shell glasses smiled. "This is fun. First Margaret's win, and now we get to meet Pickles."

Margaret raised one eyebrow. Not seeing any snacks nearby, she returned to napping. Several people walked by and congratulated her.

When Margaret's entourage finally reached the table, Duncan smiled at the young woman with long black hair. "Do you mind if we get a picture?" Duncan asked, placing a Pickles' calendar on the table for an autograph.

Evie pulled out her phone and snapped photos.

The pug sat on top of the table. Pickles glanced around at all the people.

"Not a problem," the woman said as she signed Pickles's name and drew a pawprint next to it.

"Thanks," Duncan said. "Now one more with Delanie and Margaret." He picked up the bulldog, and everyone scooched in close for a group shot.

"Oh, congratulations on your win. She's adorable as a sleuth," Pickles's friend said.

Duncan beamed. "Delanie and I work for Falcon Investigations, so the costume seemed perfect."

When they left the table, Delanie said, "I'm going to head out soon. I need to catch up on some email and invoices. You all in the office tomorrow?"

Duncan nodded. "I think we'll be leaving soon, too. This is more excitement than Margaret's had in a while. She'll probably go to bed early. I'm going back to work on our social media sites. Margaret Thatcher Reynolds, dog sleuth."

Evie giggled.

CHAPTER TWO

Delanie's phone rang the next morning while she was in line at the dry cleaners. She paid the clerk and cradled the phone between her ear and her shoulder. "Falcon Investigations. How may I help you?"

"Hello, this is Elise Childress, and I desperately need your help. Could you meet me today?"

"Hello, Ms. Childress. What do you need help with?"

The woman's voice cracked. "It's about my dog. He's missing, and I'm beside myself." She sniffed. "I saw, I guess it's your partner, on the news this morning with his dog. He was talking about your company. And I thought maybe you all could help me. I liked the bulldog in the Sherlock costume."

"How long has your dog been gone?"

"Two days. And he's not lost. I received a ransom notice yesterday." She sobbed in the phone. "Can you help me?"

"Of course. Where is a convenient place for you to meet?"

"I live near Short Pump. How about the Cheesecake Factory at one? I have some shopping to do."

"I'll see you then." Delanie ended the call.

She punched the contact for Duncan.

"What's up?" he asked.

"I got a call from a prospective client. She saw you all on TV this morning. Her dog is missing."

"I'll get Margaret right on it," he said, snickering. "We're finding lost dogs now?"

"He was taken. She said she received a ransom note. I'll meet her and get the details. I'm heading over there now."

About thirty minutes ahead of her appointment, she circled half the mall before finding a parking spot. Delanie wandered through the outdoor mall and window shopped at an eclectic jewelry store.

She glanced at her watch and walked with purpose to the restaurant. Inside the lobby, Delanie found a seat on a vinyl bench, checked her email, and glanced at the door out of the corner of her eye.

A tall woman in a black and white herringbone jacket entered and hurried over to the hostess stand. "I'm meeting someone, is she here yet?"

Delanie stood and said, "Ms. Childress? I'm Delanie Fitzgerald."

"So nice to meet you," she said, shaking hands. Then to the hostess, "We'll need a table for two, please. I'd like to sit by the window."

After they were seated in a booth next to a large, plate glass window, Delanie said, "How can my partner and I help you?"

"It's Sid. He's missing. I came home two days ago, and I couldn't find him. The housekeeper didn't remember seeing him that morning. I was frantic all night. Then I found a note in the mailbox the next morning."

"Did you call the police?"

"No. The note said not to. It said we have Sid and to wait for further instructions."

"Have you received further instructions?"

The woman's eyes teared up, and she shook her head. Delanie pulled her portfolio out as the waitress arrived.

Elise Childress dabbed her eyes. "I'll have hot tea with milk and a Caesar salad." She waved her hand around, and her diamond rings sparkled under the glass pendant lights.

"I'll have a glass of iced tea." When the waitress returned to the kitchen, Delanie continued, "Who else had access to him?"

"I live alone. Rita, my housekeeper, is there most days. The lawn service was there that morning, but they're outside a couple of days a week. They never come in the house. And Sid is never allowed outside by himself."

"What's the name of the lawn company?"

"Ace Lawn Care. I've used them for years with no problems," Elise said.

"Any idea how the dognapper got to Sid?" Delanie asked Elise, who stared out the large window at shoppers.

"Nope. He never leaves the home unless he's with me or Rita. The groomer and his trainer come to the house, but they haven't been by in a while." She paused and twisted the rings on her hands. "My guess is that Rita was careless and left the door unlocked, and someone took advantage of the situation."

The waitress brough over Elise's lunch and the drinks. While Elise ate, Delanie questioned her about details about the day Sid had disappeared. She jotted notes on her legal pad.

When Elise paused, Delanie pulled out her standard contract and pricing sheet and slid it across the table. "This is our contract and fee listing,"

Elise rummaged through her beige Chanel tote for a pen. She signed and passed the contract back to the private investigator. She dug deeper into her purse and pulled out a checkbook. Her pen scratched as she signed the check with a flourish worthy of John Hancock.

"When would be a convenient time to see your home?" Delanie asked.

"I'm headed there next. You can follow me. It's right across the way." Elise pointed toward West Broad Street and in the same motion waved the waitress over for the check. When it arrived, she placed a platinum credit card on the tray.

It was a shame no one enjoyed a slice of cheesecake.

When the waitress returned with the receipt, Delanie followed her new client to the sidewalk. "I'm over there in the white Mercedes. I'll wait to back out until I see you," she said, turning on her heels and striding to her car.

Delanie hopped in her Mustang and retraced her path to Elise Childress's large sedan. She left space for the woman to back out and followed her to the Wellesley neighborhood. Delanie admired the large McMansions on postage stamp-sized lots. Several houses had lawn crews clipping and raking. Perfectly manicured. Elise pulled into the driveway of a large home on a cul-de-sac at the back of the neighborhood. A royal blue Volkswagen Beetle sat at the curb. Delanie pulled in behind the Mercedes and recorded the license plates of both cars.

Once in the house, Elise said, "We can talk in here." She pointed to the front room. Oil paintings of miniature schnauzers and standard poodles dominated the back wall of the tastefully decorated room. "That's Sid," she said, pointing to the portrait on the end. "He comes from a long line of champions. His father was Oisin Luck of the Irish. He's a standard white French poodle."

Delanie nodded, wondering how a French poodle ended up with an Irish name. "Do you have the note?"

"Let me get it and some pictures of him," Elise said.

She returned a few minutes later and sank in the pale, yellow armchair next to the matching loveseat where Delanie perched herself on the edge with her portfolio in her lap. "Here." She handed Delanie several photos and a note printed in black ink on letter-sized paper.

I have your dog, so don't call the cops if you know what's good for you. Wait for instuccions. Two sentences and a typo. Delanie pinched the edges of the paper, trying not to add any new fingerprints. She took a picture of it with her phone.

"You may want to put this in a folder or a paper bag for the police," Delanie said.

"Oh, I'm not contacting the police. That's why I called you. I don't want them to do anything to harm Sid. You can help me find him. He's not an ordinary dog. He's a champion."

"Have you received any other contact from the dognappers?"

Elise shook her head and wiped a tear that escaped the corner of her eye.

"Do you have security cameras?" Delanie asked.

"I do, but they were off," Elise replied with a sheepish look. "I turned them off because the lawn service was working, and it blows up my phone with alerts when they're cutting grass and pulling weeds. I guess I forgot to turn them back on," she said, her voice trailing off.

A vacuum's loud hum echoed through the house.

Elise bellowed, "Rita! Not now! We're trying to talk in here. Puh-leeze! Rita!" When there was no response, she leapt from the chair and stomped into the next room. The vacuum stopped, and Elise huffed as she returned to her seat.

"Sometimes," Elise said, rolling her eyes. "Where were we? Oh, yes. I was about to tell you about life on the circuit. My dad showed dogs, so I grew up at dog shows. My late husband George bred dogs for many years, and then he moved over to the adjudication side of the business. He liked schnauzers. I always had poodles. Right now, Sid is the only one left. His lineage and awards will make him highly sought after. When he retires from the ring, he'll command top stud fees."

Delanie jotted notes as Rita entered the room. Her shoulders were slightly hunched. "May I get you all anything?" she asked, looking down at the thick, white carpet.

"Would you like anything to drink?" Elise said to Delanie. When the private investigator shook her head, Elise said, "No, Rita. Thank you."

The woman in the gray and white housekeeping uniform backed out of the room and retreated down the hallway.

"Is there anyone you suspect or anyone you've had issues with?" Delanie asked.

"No, not really. The dog competition circuit is a small world. Everybody knows everybody. They're usually friendly, but they can get catty and competitive during shows. That's normal. Most are professionals, except for Sven Donaldson. He's slimy, and I wouldn't put it past him to do something to ensure that his dogs win," she said, looking down at her manicured ruby red nails. "They all know that this is an expensive and all-consuming part of our lives. I've given a lot of blood, sweat, and tears over the years. Sid is my world. I can't imagine life without him. If it turns out to be someone on the circuit, I will lose my mind."

"What does the competition entail?" Delanie asked.

Elise stood and leaned against the couch. "Dogs are judged

according to how well they conform to their breed's standards. It's not like a beauty pageant where contestants compete with each other. Sid had the right temperament and all the requirements of his breed. It helped that both of his parents were top of the line, too. They represented the breed well. Simply the best." Elise beamed and waved her hand around as she spoke.

"Do you have a way to identify your dog?"

The woman looked down her nose. "I know my dog. But he's chipped, if that's what you're asking. And his DNA is on file when we registered him. I can prove it's him."

"Very good. My partner and I will do our research and have a progress report for you daily. Please let me know immediately if you hear anything from the dognappers."

The woman nodded. Delanie handed her a business card and followed her to the foyer. "Thank you," Elise said. "I don't know what I'll do if I don't get Sid back."

"May I have a few minutes with Rita?" Delanie asked, taking a step toward the kitchen.

A puzzled look crossed Elise's brow. "If you think it's important." She rose and pointed toward the kitchen.

Delanie wandered into what looked like a set on a cooking show. Rita turned and stared at Delanie.

"Hi, Rita. Ms. Childress has hired me to find Sid. Could you tell me about the day you discovered him missing?"

"Uh," the woman said, clutching the marble top of the island that separated them.

"Speak up," Elise demanded, standing behind Delanie and glaring at the housekeeper.

"I didn't realize he was gone. Not until Ms. Childress called me at home. It's a big house. Sometimes he's in his room when I'm working," Rita said, her voice just above a whisper.

"Anything else you remember?" Delanie asked.

The woman shook her head and looked down at her hands.

After a long pause, Elise interrupted with, "She didn't have any answers when I asked her about Sid." The older woman rolled her eyes.

"We'll do our best to find him. If you think of anything else, please don't hesitate to call me at any time," Delanie said.

Delanie sat in her car in the driveway. *How was she going to find this dog?* She put the car in reverse and pushed the button on the steering wheel to call Duncan.

"Hey, did you get the scoop on the dognapping?" he asked.

"Yes. And I have no idea where to start on this. Sid is a show dog who's worth quite a lot of money. Our new client Elise insists that she's not going to involve the police. Something's not right about all of this. I need to do some poking around."

"What's next, Nancy Drew?" Duncan asked as he crunched something that sounded like ice or rocks.

"I'm heading to the office to work on my case file. Maybe something will jump out and point me in the right direction."

"Margaret and I missed lunch. How about if I call in an order at the Golden Panda, and you pick it up. We'll help you look over your notes."

"Deal. See you in about forty minutes." She disconnected the call.

It took longer than Delanie expected, but she finally made it to the office with the food. Margaret, sniffing the air, followed her down the hall to the conference room where Duncan had already set up shop.

Delanie set her messenger bag in the chair next to her and dropped the paper bags on the table. "Do you have a drink?"

He shook his head, and she headed to the kitchenette for two cans of Coke. When she returned, he had all the takeout containers spread out on the table. He tossed her plastic utensils and a fortune cookie.

She tore into her sesame chicken and fried rice. Duncan made a small plate for Margaret and then dug into his beef and broccoli.

"So, what's giving you pause about the new client?" he asked between bites.

"She's adamant about not involving the police, but in the next breath, she tells me how wonderful and valuable this dog is. She seems concerned or sad, but then she flips to indifferent in two seconds flat. If it were me or you, I know we'd be doing anything to get Margaret back."

"What have you got so far?" He shoveled beef and broccoli and steamed rice into his mouth. Margaret had already wolfed down hers and looked around for more.

Delanie fished her legal pad and laptop out of her bag. "I have two license plates I'd like you to check. One is the client, Elise Childress's, and the other is for her housekeeper Rita. See what you can find on them." She jotted the plate numbers on a piece of paper and passed it to her partner. "She mentioned a lawn service and another dog owner, Sven Donaldson. Can you check on him for me?"

"Let's see what's out there," he said, wiping his hands on his jeans. He opened his laptop, covered with colorful stickers on the lid that advertised everything from cool software vendors to Bigfoot. Delanie finished her lunch while he poked around in the dark secret places of the internet.

"Will you guys eat the leftovers if I put them in the fridge?" she asked. Duncan nodded.

By the time she put the food away and took the trash to the dumpster, Duncan had started to flesh out profiles for both of the women she'd met today.

"Okay, here's what I got so far. Elise Childress, formerly Winston, has been in the dog show business all her life. Her husband, George, raised miniature and full-sized schnauzers. He was also a renowned judge on the dog show circuit. Let's see. He died about ten years ago. She's still active on show dog websites. It looks like Sid has his own website and Facebook page with over eight thousand followers. The other license plate belongs to Rita Meecham. Here's her address. I didn't see much on her." He passed her a sticky with the address.

Delanie opened a new file and keyed in all the information she had. When she finished, she Googled dognappings. At least four mystery novels with that plot popped up in her search. She didn't see any recent online articles on dog abductions, just advertisements for pet micro-chipping. She closed the browser. "Elise lives alone. She said that a crew from Ace Landscaping was there the day the dog disappeared. Can you check them out?

When I was there, Rita was the only other person in the house."

"Security cameras?"

"Elise turned them off because they were cutting grass outside, and she didn't like all the alerts on her phone. Functioning cameras would have been helpful."

"So, what's next?" he asked.

"Not a lot of clues. I need to think about this one for a while. I'll stake out Elise's residence and see if I uncover anything. If you have any brainstorms, I'm open."

CHAPTER THREE

Delanie settled in to read through her notes and waited to see what would happen.woke up the next morning and glanced at her clock. It was eight minutes after eleven. She had stayed up late checking on the dog show circuit. She emailed every shelter and dog rescue site she should find with an alert on Sid. No responses yet. After a shower and an espresso, Delanie grabbed her camera and notes and drove to the dog owner's home. She parked at the edge of the cul-de-sac where she could see the front of the house without being too conspicuous. Rita's blue Bug sat at the curb.

A little after one, Elise's Mercedes backed out of the garage and zoomed out of the neighborhood.

Delanie's mind started to wander. She counted trees and wrought iron lampposts. She reached for her phone and punched in Duncan's contact.

"Hey, dude," she said. "What's up?"

"Making peanut butter and marshmallow spread sandwiches," he said. "What are you doing?"

"I'm staking out Elise Childress's house to see what's going on. I was hoping you had more on their backgrounds."

"I'll do some more digging this afternoon." It sounded like Duncan was chewing on something. "I contacted the lawn company. They're used to working with wealthy clients. All of the workers have background, security, and credit checks. The guys on Elise's crew finished her yard and did two others in another ritzy neighborhood that day. They all left together in the company truck."

"Hmmm. A group alibi," she muttered.

"I found your Sven Donaldson. Don't think he did it. He passed away a week ago. He was showing dogs at some event and died of a heart attack. Lots of witnesses. You find anything interesting? Having fun?" he asked.

"Loads. I'm trying to stay focused. It's like watching paint dry."

Duncan laughed and ended the call. Delanie scanned the street and the neighbors' front yards. A dog barked and distracted her.

Rita walked around the house with her purse and a shopping bag on her arm. She hurried to her car, slammed the door, and gunned the engine. Delanie barely had time to start her car to tail the housekeeper.

Delanie hung back but kept the little blue car in sight. She followed the housekeeper out of the swanky neighborhood to Broad Street. Rita stomped on the accelerator and played Frogger, hopping to empty spots across three lanes of traffic. Rita ducked off the highway onto the 288 South exit and floored it on the open road. Delanie mashed the accelerator, and her black Mustang growled.

After they crossed the James River and headed into Chesterfield County, Rita zipped off at the Lucks Lane exit and traversed a warren of neighborhood streets. She pulled into a long driveway on Darrell Drive and screeched the brakes. The driveway ended at the white garage door with chipped paint. The housekeeper climbed out of the small car and entered a gray house with wood siding. A double garage door that had seen better days and a smaller door fronted the road. Overgrown bushes stood like sloppy sentries at the end of the asphalt drive. Delanie parked at the corner. The shrubs provided great cover for her spying. She texted Duncan the address and photos of the house.

Then she settled in for more snooping. At least, there was new scenery to look at here. At the point when she was struggling to stay awake, her phone dinged.

The house belongs to Rita Meecham and Ricky Steeples.

Thanks. Who's Ricky?

Still digging, Duncan texted.

Delanie added the scant information to her notes. A door slammed and a few seconds later, Rita jumped in her car and sped down the long driveway in reverse. The little car lurched when she shifted to drive. Rita tore out of the neighborhood. Delanie did a U-turn and followed behind her.

The Beetle zipped through the neighborhood streets and back roads until Rita emerged at Courthouse Road and cut off several cars to turn into the Food Lion parking lot. Delanie paused to let the other cars pass before she turned and found a spot near Rita's car. Delanie tailed Rita through the produce section. The private investigator grabbed a cart and pretended to shop. On the next aisle, she compared labels while Rita grabbed items off the shelf. The other woman shopped as fast as she drove.

Delanie put a couple of items in her cart and strolled to the next aisle. Rita, already at the end, rounded the corner and moved on to the paper products. She skipped a few aisles and made a beeline for the frozen foods. She strode down the aisle to pick up milk, eggs, beer, and shredded cheese. She bypassed the bakery and zipped into the shortest checkout line. Delanie ditched her basket and walked around the manager's office and out the front door. She had the Mustang started by the time Rita exited and loaded four bags of groceries in her car. Rita returned the cart and within seconds, her car headed out of the parking lot.

Delanie dodged slower cars to keep the blue Beetle in sight.

Rita returned to the home on Darrell Drive. It took two trips to haul the groceries inside. This time, an older truck, parked in the driveway, blocked the double garage door. Delanie jotted down the license plate number.

Delanie surveyed the backyard, filled with mature oak trees and overgrown crepe myrtles that dotted the perimeter. Overgrown briars covered a rusty, metal shed. She wanted to sneak around the house, but there was no cover. Anyone at a back window would spot her.

Giving up on her stakeout, Delanie drove back to the office

to see what Duncan had uncovered. He and Margaret were headed out in his bright yellow Camaro.

She climbed out of her car as Duncan and Margaret backed out of a nearby parking spot. He rolled down the window and idled. Margaret jumped in Duncan's lap and stuck her head out the window. Delanie leaned over to talk, but she didn't get to get too close. Margaret was the slobber queen with what seemed like a three-foot tongue.

"Where are y'all headed?" she asked.

"Home. I emailed you some information. Elise Childress came from money, but she inherited more when her husband died. The house is paid off. She travels a lot to dog shows. She likes to shop and eat out a lot. And you already know what she drives. Her housekeeper is thirty-five. She's been employed by Ms. Childress for about three years. She lives in Chesterfield County with her boyfriend, Ricky Steeples, who works part-time as a house painter. And he has an online gamer's name, Slick Rick."

Delanie raised her eyebrows. "And drives an old red truck."

"Yep," he said, flipping through a file on his phone. "Ricky is younger than Rita. According to the tax records, she lived in the house before him. A Jerry Callo was on the deed in 2008. That name disappeared in 2010."

"Thanks. You always find good stuff. I have no idea where this dog is. And there has been no other communication from the napper. My searches in the dog show world and shelters didn't turn up anything."

"Well, I want us to find the dog. I would be lost without Margaret. And you saw from the crowds at Strut Your Mutt how important dogs are to their peeps."

Delanie smiled.

Duncan put his car in reverse and backed out slowly. "See you tomorrow."

She waved. When his taillights faded in the distance, she climbed back in the Mustang, opting for dinner in a bag since she wasn't in the mood to cook anything.

While in the drive-thru, Delanie told her car to call Elise.

After three rings, her client answered with a chipper, "Hello."

"Ms. Childress. This is Delanie Fitzgerald. I wanted to check in to see if you've heard further from the dognappers."

"No, nothing." The older woman sniffed.

"Okay, please let me know as soon as you do. Time is of the essence. Also, did you turn your cameras back on?"

After a long pause, the woman replied. "I'll go turn them on now."

"Sounds good. You never know what they'll pick up."

Elise said, "Yes, you're right," before the call disconnected.

Delanie finished her dinner in a bag. Then she drew a hot, soapy bath. Bubbles and her favorite mystery. Perfect relaxation. By the time the water started to cool off, she had a thought about Rita and Ricky. She toweled off and slid on her fluffy pink robe and matching slippers. Delanie padded to her bedroom and spread her notes across the bed.

Pulling up Duncan's email, she scanned the details and updated her notes. She could either poke around Rita's house when she wasn't there or try to interview her at Elise's during work hours. Something about Rita bothered her. The housekeeper almost cowered when her employer was around.

Delanie made a plan to stake out Elise's house again tomorrow in hopes of getting a chance to talk to Rita. Maybe she'd be willing to talk more if Elise wasn't within earshot.

CHAPTER FOUR

The next morning, Delanie rose with the sun that peeked through her window and surprised herself with her domestic productivity. She made the bed, did a load of laundry, and hung up all the clothes draped on her chair. After her shower and a second cup of coffee, she headed out to see what she'd find at Elise's house. As each day passed, she worried more and more about the dog. Why was the napper waiting? She would be beside herself if something had happened to Margaret. While she wasn't much of a guard dog, she had alerted them when there'd been a snake in the office last fall. That made her a hero in Delanie's book.

Delanie drove across town and found a snooping spot down the street from Elise's house. The blue Bug sat in its usual spot. About forty-five minutes into her spying, the garage door opened, and Elise backed her Mercedes down the driveway.

When she was sure it was clear, Delanie walked up the driveway and rang the doorbell. Something rustled, and then Rita opened the large wooden door a crack.

"Hi, Rita. I'm Delanie Fitzgerald."

"I remember you. Ms. Childress isn't here right now. May I take a message?" she asked, looking down at her feet.

"I was hoping to get some information. We didn't get to talk much the other day," Delanie said.

"I'm not supposed to let anyone in when Ms. Childress isn't here."

"Well, we can talk on the porch," Delanie said, offering a

compromise.

"I guess," the other woman said. She opened the door a little wider and stepped out on the porch. "Let's take a walk." She looked over her shoulder at the camera on the porch and up and down the street before she descended the steps.

Delanie walked down the driveway beside the woman in her gray dress. She didn't know housekeepers today wore uniforms like 1970s TV maids.

At the mailbox, Rita broke the silence. "What do you want?"

Delanie cleared her throat. "I was hoping you could tell me what happened when Ms. Childress's dog went missing."

Rita paused. "I washed and dried all the sheets and towels that morning. Then I dusted and ran the vacuum. Sid, that's his name, doesn't like the vacuum. He usually hides under one of the beds. I didn't think anything about it. He usually comes out when the noise stops. I don't remember seeing him the rest of the day. But that's not unusual. He has his own room upstairs. He hangs out there or in the sunroom. I left at my usual time even though Ms. Childress wasn't back from her appointments. Then Ms. Childress called me in a panic that night. She wanted to know what happened to her baby."

"Then what?" Delanie asked, leaning on the brick and metal mailbox.

"She kinda implied that I had left a door open, and he'd run away." The woman looked down at her chapped hands.

"Did you?"

"Of course not. I know he's not allowed outside. I'm always careful to lock all the doors." A pained look crossed the woman's face. She brushed a strand of hair that escaped from her loose ponytail.

"Anything else you can think of?" Delanie asked.

"She got a ransom note the next day."

"How did it arrive?"

"It was in the newspaper slot under the mailbox. I pulled it out when I got the mail. I thought it was a flyer or something," Rita said.

"Do you know of anyone who dislikes Ms. Childress or who

would want to steal Sid?"

The housekeeper laughed and caught herself. "She had spats with people on the dog show circuit. I'd overhear her on the phone sometimes. Ms. Childress can be abrasive and kinda fierce."

"Any names?"

"No. It's hard not to eavesdrop when she's so loud, but I try not to pay attention to the details."

"She has cameras. Is it unusual to have them turned off?"

"No," Rita said. "She doesn't like it alerting her phone when the groundskeepers are working in the yard. She often turns them off." The woman twisted a button on the front of her blouse as she talked. "Plus, they only cover the porch and the backyard."

"Can you think of anyone who would want to take her dog?"

"No. Sorry. He was a sweet dog. I hope you can find him. I told her to pay the ransom and follow the demands, but she didn't listen to me. She waited and then called you."

Delanie smiled, trying to make the woman feel comfortable. "Is there anything you can tell me about Sid?"

She wrinkled her nose and hesitated. "He's a dog." She pulled at her button again. "He's a big, white poodle. His face and paws are fuzzy, and his body is always clipped short. Oh, he had on a red collar with his tags and charms. He's kinda prissy when he walks."

"Do you know if she's going to pay the money?"

The housekeeper paused. "I heard her tell someone on the phone that it would take her a few days to get that kind of money. And that was the day you came over."

"Thanks. I appreciate your time. If you remember anything else, please contact me."

The woman nodded and turned back to the house. Rita entered through the front door before Delanie retrieved her car.

The sun had warmed the interior of the Mustang. She opened the windows and found a station on the radio and rocked out to AC/DC. Delanie followed her path from yesterday, but at a slower pace than what Rita drove.

Thirty minutes later, she sat across the street from Rita and

Ricky's house. No red truck. The house looked empty, but it was hard to tell from the side. Delanie slid her phone in her pocket and pulled her magic cap with its hidden camera from her sleuthing bag in the trunk. Then she rummaged around for a clipboard and a lanyard with a name tag on it

She walked around a dirt path to the front of the house, studying the skinny front porch and white railing and the dirty, plate glass window. Inside, there was a front room with a modular black leather couch and two end tables. A standup piano sat by itself on the long wall, and a giant flat screen TV took up the majority of the opposite wall. All of the flat surfaces were covered with magazines, unopened mail, snack bags, a gaming console, and beer cans. Delanie could see an eating area with a colonial oak table and four chairs near a kitchen area in the back of the house. Plates and boxes covered the table's surface. Rita must be too tired after work to clean here, too.

Delanie walked around the property. The overgrown backyard would look spooky in the dark. Sticks, leaves, and out of control bushes bordered the perimeter of the property, and an older aluminum shed with a rusted roof sat alone in the far corner of the yard.

Not finding much in the backyard, Delanie returned to the front and looked around the neighborhood. A tiny bungalow with better curb appeal and a car in the driveway sat across the street from Rita's house. She rang the doorbell and waited. After the second ring, Delanie heard shuffling and the door opened.

An older woman in sunflower stretch pants and an oversized green sweater opened the door. "Yes?"

"Hi, I'm Marie Kellogg, and I'm doing a survey for the county. It's time for Chesterfield's annual pet census." Delanie smiled and held up her clipboard.

"I've never heard of that." The woman furrowed her brows and squinted.

"It's relatively new. As a pilot group this year, the county picked several neighborhoods for volunteers to inventory the number of pets. This is my area. Could you tell me how many pets you have?"

"A cat. It's a Persian, and her name is Princess Zelda."

"Aww," Delanie said, marking the paper on her clipboard. "And your house number is 13555?"

"Yes," the woman said, looking up and down the street.

"What about your neighbors?" Delanie pointed to the red house next door. "Do they have any pets?"

"The Phillipses live there. The kids have some kind of gerbils or guinea pigs. Their dog got hit by a car last summer."

"Oh, that's sad." Delanie scribbled fake notes on her clipboard. "And what about that gray house across the street?"

"Rita lives there with her lazy boyfriend."

Delanie frowned and waited.

The woman twisted her wedding rings and continued, "He can't be bothered to do anything. Rita works herself to death, and then she comes home and cuts the grass. I wouldn't let his lazy butt sit around all day and play those stupid video games. For Pete's sake, he's a grown man. He could at least do something to help her when he's home so much." The woman glanced over at Rita's house and scowled.

"Some people," Delanie said quietly. "Do they have any pets?"

"They had two big dogs that barked a lot at night. One's a lab mix, and the other is some monstrous thing that gallops. I think the big one that I called a horse ran away. They had a couple of cats, but they've disappeared over the years. So now, put them down for one dog. Oh, but I did see him outside with another dog the other day. Maybe they got a new one. Just what they need. Rita has enough to take care of with that oversized man child."

"Maybe they have guests?"

"Doubtful. It's rare that they have visitors. He's not friendly. He yells a lot."

"Do you know what kind of dog the new one was?"

"I don't know. It was around dusk, and I happened to see them outside when I was washing dishes. I don't see that well without my glasses. It wasn't a tiny dog. Maybe one of those labradoodle things." The woman looked up and down the street.

"The Marshalls on the corner have three cats and an old beagle, named Max. He gets out from time to time and sits on my porch. He's harmless."

"Well, Mrs. Uh, Mrs...."

"Campbell," the woman interjected.

"Mrs. Campbell, you've been most helpful. Thank you so much for your time."

"Good luck. But I think it sounds like a dumb way for the county to spend my tax dollars," she grumbled as she shut the door.

Delanie jogged back to her car and threw her hat and clipboard on the passenger seat. Butterflies awakened in her stomach. She needed to see the new dog at Ricky and Rita's house. She slid in the front seat as the red truck rumbled down the street and into the Rita's driveway. It belched and ticked when the man turned it off. He grabbed a bag of dog food and a case of beer and slammed the door. Leaving the dog food by the door, he fished in his pocket for keys and opened the smaller garage door. He returned a few minutes later for the large blue bag with a German shepherd on it.

She put her hat back on and turned on the camera. Delanie pulled out her clipboard and trudged up to the front porch and rang the bell. Heavy footsteps echoed outside the door. A bear of a man who resembled a lumber jack in jeans and a red t-shirt yanked open the door. His receding hairline and a scruffy brown beard made him look older than he probably was.

Delanie smiled her sweetest smile and said, "Hi, I'm Marie Kellogg, and I'm doing a survey for the county. Could you tell me how many pets you have?"

"None," he said gruffly as a dog barked somewhere in the house. Before the man could speak, a large, white dog bounded to the door. A yellow lab followed close behind it. The yellow dog barked, and the man nudged it away with his foot. The white poodle sat on the mat and dusted the floor with his wagging pompom tail.

Delanie looked down at the poodle and rubbed behind its ears. "You're so cute." She made sure to capture the dog with her hidden camera. The other dog lost interest and wandered toward the kitchen.

"Oh, uh him. He belongs to my sister. We're watching him while they're in Hawaii. The other dog belongs to my brother."

"Well, this guy is adorable. Aren't you snoogie wookums?" she asked as she bent down and petted the dog. "What's his name?"

"Uh, Fifi," the man said.

"Any other pets?" she asked, rubbing the dog behind the ears. No collar or tags.

"Nope," said the man, shifting his weight from one foot to the other. "I just got home from work. I need to do stuff."

"I'm sorry. I didn't mean to keep you. Fifi here is so cute and well behaved. I could eat him up. Thanks for your time," she said, standing. When he shut the door firmly, she retreated to her car and turned off the camera.

She started the car and told the radio to call Duncan.

"How's the sleuthing?" her partner asked.

"I found the dog. Ricky called him Fifi."

"Ha. That's great news. Where?" he asked.

"It's at the housekeeper's house with the boyfriend."

"What are you planning?"

"Not sure yet," she said. "If I wait, they could move the dog. I'm guessing that Rita and Ricky are both in on it. I'm debating whether to call my brother Steve at work or confront the housekeeper at our client's house."

"I'd go with Steve. If you confront them, there's a risk that the boyfriend will hightail it with the dog."

"You're probably right. I wanted to wrap it up myself, but I did the door-to-door survey thing to get a look at the house, so he could ID me now. Although, he's not the brightest bulb. Thanks, Duncan."

"No problem. I'm always here for you," he said, clicking off.

On the drive home, Delanie had second thoughts about her plan for Sid. She knew the poodle at Rita's house was Sid, but she needed proof if she planned to call the police whether or not Elise Childress approved. Delanie's eldest brother, Steve, had been on the Chesterfield County police force for years and was her best law enforcement resource. What Elise Childress didn't know wouldn't hurt her.

CHAPTER FIVE

Delanie woke up to a loud buzzing. It paused and continued. She shook off the haziness from a dream and sat up in her dark bedroom. Her phone, buzzing on the nightstand, lit up the room. Five thirty-five in the morning.

"She fumbled with the buttons. "Hello," she said.

"Delanie. This is Elise Childress. I found another note. This one was mailed."

"What does it say?"

"We want $100,000 by tomorrow, or you won't see the dog ever again. Put it in a bag and have your maid take it to Rockwood Park at 4 PM."

"No date?"

"No. I have no idea when I'm supposed to send the money," Elise said. "It came to my home address. To make things worse, Rita didn't show up for work yesterday. And she didn't answer my call. Her timing is terrible. I found this when I sorted the mail this morning. What if I missed the deadline?" she wailed.

"When was this postmarked?"

Something rattled. "Two days ago in Richmond," Elise said.

"I wonder if the thieves know it took two days to arrive in the mail?"

Elise let out a heavy sigh. "They can't be that stupid, can they? They were the doofuses who dropped it in the mail."

"Put it in a folder with the envelope. Do you want to call the police?"

"No. I don't want them to hurt Sid." Elise sniffed. "Maybe

215

it's not too late."

"Do you expect Rita to come to work today?"

"I expected her yesterday. This isn't like her. She's usually more responsible than this. If she doesn't show up, I don't know what I'll do about the money exchange. I have no way of communicating with those horrible people."

"Okay, I have a few leads that I'm working on for your case. I'll be over later with a strategy."

"I'm headed to the gym now. I should be at home about ten after I work out, get coffee, and do some shopping. See you." Elise ended the call. Her mood seemed to change every twenty seconds.

Delanie hoped an espresso and a hot shower would help her get rid of the foggy-headedness. She needed to come up with a plan to get Sid. A little voice in the back of her head reminded her to let the police handle this, but she shook it off and rummaged through her closet for an outfit. She worried about Sid. She had to rescue him. Rita and Ricky probably felt cornered, and Delanie didn't know how desperate they were. And where was Rita? She had to find out.

After a shower and breakfast, she picked up her laptop and purse. She dialed Duncan as she backed down the driveway.

"What's up?" he asked after a couple of rings.

"Elise got another ransom note. This one came in the mail. The napper wants one hundred thousand by four o'clock. The hitch is that it was mailed two days ago. And it didn't say what day to make the drop."

"Wow. I'd give better directions if I was the dognapper," Duncan said. "And I wouldn't have sent it by snail mail. Someone needs a better plan."

"I want to make sure nothing's happened to Sid. And the note wanted the maid to drop the money in a park. Elise said Rita didn't show up for work yesterday. She showed more anger about the inconvenience of Rita's absence than concern for her housekeeper."

"What's your plan?"

Delanie let out a breath she didn't realize she was holding. "I know where Sid is. I could wait for Ricky and Rita to leave and get the dog. Does your vet microchip pets?"

"Yep. Margaret has one."

"If I get Sid, can we swing by and get him scanned? I want to be one hundred percent sure before we bring in the police."

"That's no problem. We've been going to Dr. Pete for years. They'll squeeze us in."

"I'm headed over to Rita's."

"Be careful. Call me if you need me. Margaret and I are great backup."

"Thanks. I'll let you know what happens."

Delanie ran through the doughnut shop drive-thru for another shot of caffeine courage. By the time the hot, sweet drink started to take effect, Delanie had formulated a plan. She'd watch the house and look for an opportunity to grab Sid. If things went south, she'd call her brother for police backup. He wouldn't be happy with her involvement, but she'd deal with that after Sid was safe.

She drove the backroads to Rita's house and parked in front of a blue, two-story down the street. Ricky's red truck and Rita's blue Bug sat next to each other on the cracked driveway in front of the garage.

Delanie heard a door slam. Ricky threw two trash bags in the back of his pickup and jumped in the cab. The engine sputtered and stalled. After the third try, it came to life, and he roared out the driveway in a cloud of blue-gray smoke.

Quiet returned to the street. A few cars drove by, but there was no sign of Rita. If she was at home, maybe she could convince her to return Sid. Delanie pocketed her phone and jogged to the front door. She banged and paused. Dogs barked somewhere inside the home.

After several knocks and no response, Delanie made her way around the perimeter of the house. The garage's side door was also locked. She walked through the dead crabgrass and around a flowerbed that hadn't been tended in years,

She looked in a window at the far end of the house. Through the dirty glass, she could see a large unmade bed and a pile of clothes on the floor. No sign of anyone. Getting braver, she walked around and peeked in the kitchen window. The table looked like it did before, with the counters and sink stacked high with dishes, cups, and pans.

With no signs of life in the house except the dogs, Delanie tried the two doors at the back of the house. She turned the knob on the smaller door. It creaked. After a good tug, the door opened to reveal a built-in shed about the size of a walk-in closet.

She got a whiff of the closed in air and stepped back. It smelled like a cross between a skunk and a lot of mildew. A car door slammed nearby.

Delanie's pulse raced. She had to hide if it was Ricky or Rita.

Delanie stepped inside and pulled the door almost closed. A tiny crack of light illuminated the edge of the door, but it wasn't good for seeing what was happening outside. Delanie strained to listen for any approaching noise.

The stench inside the little shed was almost unbearable. It seemed to get worse the longer that she was in there. Delanie waited about ten minutes. She didn't hear any other sounds outside.

She pushed the door open slightly. Not hearing anything, she pushed it open more and stuck her head out. No signs of life. The light flooded in the little room, but it wasn't enough to see all the contents. She flipped the switch, and a single hanging bulb lit up the space.

Delanie stifled a scream. Not three feet from where she had been hiding, two sneakers jutted out from under a beat-up blue tarp. Delanie stepped outside and leaned over. She took deep breaths until she could quell the rising bile.

She took one deep breath and let it out. Delanie wanted to run to her car, but she had to know who was in there. She pulled the edge back.

Delanie gasped. Underneath, a very dead Rita looked like she was sleeping in the shed.

Delanie took a couple of pictures. Then retreated and closed the door. She knew she needed to call the police, but the urgency to get Sid out of there before Ricky returned won out. And with

Ricky's work ethic, that could be any time. She tiptoed around the house, trying to keep her back close to the wall. At the corner, she summoned the courage to stick her head out for a quick look. No red truck. Good. She'd call the police later.

She returned to the kitchen window and whistled. Dogs barked inside, but no sign of any people.

Delanie looked around the small patio area. The biggest items were three faded plastic chairs and two hand-painted terracotta pots full of dry stalks. She spotted a pile of sidewalk pavers stacked next to the tiny cement slab.

She grabbed one and slammed it against the glass in the back door. The pane cracked. She whacked it again and then used the edge to knock out all the glass. She stood on her tiptoes and reached in to unlock the back door. This was an emergency. There was a dead body on the premises. She'd explain breaking and entering later if she had to. Delanie had to get inside and find out what happened to Rita and get Sid.

Once inside, she paused and listened. Muffled barking. She tiptoed toward the sound. One of the bedroom doors was shut. She turned the knob, and two dogs flew out, knocking her backward. The lickfest was on. A yellow lab and a standard poodle jumped on top of her for licks and pets. Delanie finally freed herself. She hugged both dogs and stood. After more pats, she looked around for a leash. Not finding one, she put her hands on the poodle's back and led him down the hall.

"Hey, fella," she said to the lab. "I'm going to have to leave you here, but I promise I'll call someone and get them to come and get you. You're a good boy. Come on, Sid. Let's go for a ride."

At the magic "R" word, Sid lunged forward and ran toward the door. The yellow lab danced around the pair. Delanie grabbed the poodle and let him out the back door.

"Okay, we have to be quick about this." Hoping he wouldn't dart away, she led Sid around the side of the garage. She stuck her head around the corner and checked for Ricky. When the coast was clear, she led the oversized Muppet down the driveway. She clicked her key fob and opened the door. Sid jumped in the front seat. She shoved him over to the passenger seat and squeezed in.

Delanie slammed the door and got Sid settled. A noise made her look up. An old red truck puttered down the road. Delanie started the engine and threw the car in drive. She mashed the accelerator, and the car leapt forward. She sped out of the neighborhood, hoping Ricky hadn't noticed them.

When she turned the corner, she let out a sigh. But before she could call Duncan, she spotted the truck rounding the corner. She floored it and headed for Lucks Lane. Not wanting to lead him back to her office or home, she jumped on 288 and sped north. The truck tailed her about three car-lengths behind her. She wove in and out of traffic and floored it. When she could no longer see Ricky, she ducked off the nearest exit, did a U-turn and jumped back on 288 in the other direction.

She let out a deep breath when she didn't see the red truck. Her nerves got the best of her, and she checked the rearview mirror every two minutes. No sign of Ricky. She told the car, "Call Duncan."

"Morning, sunshine. What's up?"

"I found a body, grabbed the dog, and got chased by Ricky in the last hour. How's your morning going?"

"Not quite that exciting. Margaret and I are working on a website for a hair salon."

"Can you call your vet and meet me there? I need to know if this is definitely Sid." When she said his name, the poodle looked at her, and he winked. She patted him on the head.

"Sure. It's Dr. Pete's at Hull Street and Genito Road. I'll call them."

"Cool. We'll be there in about ten or fifteen minutes. We'll wait if you're not there."

"We're heading out now. See you in a few."

Delanie arrived at the strip mall and parked in front of the vet's office. A few minutes later, Duncan and Margaret pulled up in his Tweetie-bird colored Camaro. He parked next to her, and he and his sidekick jumped out. Delanie blocked Sid and helped him out of the Mustang.

They trotted across the asphalt to the vet's front door. Once inside, Duncan said to the young woman with purple hair. "Hi, I'm Duncan Reynolds, and this is Margaret. I called a few minutes ago about getting a chip read on a dog that we found. It's this poodle."

"Sure. Go on in room three. Dr. Pete or Dr. Jocelyn will be with you in a minute."

Sid hopped up on the wooden bench in the exam room while Margaret curled up under the aluminum examining table for a nap. Delanie stood next to Sid and patted his head.

The back door opened a few minutes later, and Dr. Pete walked in with a handheld device. "Hey, Duncan. Hey, Margaret. Michelle said you needed a chip scan on a lost dog."

"Yes, thanks so much," Duncan said. "This is Delanie, my partner, and we want to get the dog back to its rightful owners."

"It shouldn't take but a minute to get the info if the dog's chipped. Let's hope so." He scanned the dog's hindquarters. The device beeped. "We're in luck. He's registered. This is Sid. Oh, he has a long, full name that I can't seem to pronounce. His owner is Elise Childress." He jotted something on the back of a sticky note. "Here's the contact information."

"Okay, Sid. Let's get you to your family," Delanie said.

"How much do I owe you?" Duncan reached for his wallet.

"I'm happy to get lost dogs back to their owners. And I'm sure someone is looking for this handsome guy. See you around." Dr. Pete waved and exited through the back door.

As they made their way through the lobby, filled with several waiting patients, Duncan said, "What's the plan?"

"Can you take Sid back to either your place or the office until I can get with the police and Elise? He'll be safer there since Ricky doesn't know about you. He followed us up Route 288, but I was able to lose him in traffic."

"Okay, come on, Sid. Let's get some lunch and have a playdate with Margaret. I'll see if I can find a collar and a leash that you can borrow." Sid's ears perked up as he jumped in the passenger seat.

Margaret gave him the stink eye when Duncan put her in the back seat of the Camaro.

"Baby, it's okay. He's our guest. He can sit in your seat just this once." Duncan patted Margaret's back and kissed her boxy head.

Margaret didn't look impressed as she curled up on Duncan's jacket in the back.

"Okay. I'll take them to my house and wait to hear from you." Duncan closed his door and started the Camaro.

When she was locked inside her Mustang, Delanie dialed her brother. "Fitzgerald here."

"Hey, Steve. Can you talk?"

"What's up? I'm headed back to the office."

"I have a client whose show dog was nabbed in Henrico. She received a ransom note but didn't want to go to the police."

"And what did you do?"

"Duncan and I investigated. I found out the dog was at the woman's housekeeper's house."

"Interesting. But there's more, right?" Steve asked.

"Of course. Elise, the owner, called me last night. She got another note with instructions about having her maid leave the money at Rockwood Park. The only hitch was that it had been mailed two days ago, so she had probably missed the drop. And her maid, Rita, didn't show up for work that day."

"Where are you now?"

"At the maid's house. I waited until her boyfriend left. The woman's car was in the driveway, but there was no sign of life."

"And? There's always an and with you."

"I discovered the housekeeper covered in a painter's tarp. And I found two dogs in the house. One was Sid. We took him to the vet and had his chip read. So, it's definitely the missing dog."

"What's the address of the maid's house?"

"It's 6001 Darrell Drive near Lucks Lane."

"Got it. I'll get somebody over there. And I'm guessing you weren't invited in?"

"Nope. Not really. The body is in a little closet-like shed. The door's at the back of the house."

"Was the door unlocked?"

"The shed was. The house wasn't."

"And I'm guessing you didn't have a key."

Delanie pursed her lips and didn't respond.

He let out a loud sigh. "And you're sure it was a body."

"Yes. It wasn't a life-sized doll or a mannequin. And it had a smell. I'll text you a picture. I'm pretty sure it's Rita."

"I'll take care of it," her brother said.

"Thanks," Delanie said quietly. "I'll get the dog back to the owner. Uh, could you make sure somebody takes care of the other dog in the house. He's a nice yellow lab."

"Ten-four. See you later." Her brother ended the call.

"Sooner than you think," she muttered as she texted him the photo. She started the car and sped to Rita's house. Sid was safe, so she had some time to see what the police would do.

The street looked fairly empty. Delanie pulled in front of Mrs. Campbell's home across the street and parked at the curb. There was no sign of life at Rita's and no police activity.

Delanie skimmed her email. She looked up every time a car drove down the street.

Where were the police? She told them there was a dead body. Delanie wanted to get Sid back to Elise, but she didn't want to miss what the police discovered at the house.

After what seemed like forever, a loud engine roared. She glanced up. In her rearview mirror she spotted Ricky's truck zooming around the corner. He sped up and barreled down the neighborhood street.

Before she could start the Mustang, he slowed down. He pulled in right behind her and tapped her bumper. Delanie felt a rush of anger and then a moment of panic. What was this guy going to do? Before she could speed away, he jumped out and started pounding on her car roof and hood with his fists.

"Where's the dog? First Rita and now you! This was supposed to be easy money. Where is that stupid dog? What have you done with him?" he demanded.

Delanie started the engine as the red-faced man danced around the car and pounded on her passenger window with his palms. "Open this door and give me my dog. I want my dog," he bellowed. "You stole from me." He leaned down to look in the window and kicked the door. "Rita got all soft on me and wanted to return it so she wouldn't get fired. She threatened to call the cops. And now you stole it. What else is going to go wrong? Everything's all messed up now. I just need the dog back."

Before Delanie could pull away, the front door of the neighbor's house flew open, and Mrs. Campbell dashed down the three cement steps swinging a small weeding shovel.

"Get off my lawn, you idiot. And leave that woman alone. You have no business banging on her car and acting like a jackass." The septuagenarian swung the shovel around like a light saber.

Ricky turned and lunged at her, and she made contact with the side of his head. The large man stumbled and took a step back. Mrs. Campbell pulled the shovel back and swung again. She connected with his head again. Then for good measure, she hit him several more times. The man's eyes rolled back, and he fell backwards and hit his head on the cement driveway.

Mrs. Campbell kicked him several times with her pink bedroom slipper.

Delanie climbed out of her car as three police cruisers sped down the street with lights flashing and sirens blaring. One skidded to a stop behind the truck while another pulled in front of Delanie's car and blocked the street.

All three officers rushed over to Mrs. Campbell and the prone Ricky. "Officer, this man tried to attack this nice young woman. He was pounding on her car and threatening her. I had to stop him before he caused some real damage and hurt her. Officers, I was afraid for our lives."

A young officer reached for the shovel. "And you took care of him?"

Mrs. Campbell handed him the shovel. "Yes. I don't like lazy bullies." She crossed her arms across her chest and stared at Ricky. The officer radioed for an ambulance with his shoulder mic after he checked Ricky for a pulse.

"D, why don't you tell us what happened?" Delanie's brother asked.

Delanie spent the next ten minutes explaining the story to Mrs. Campbell.

"Oh, my stars." Mrs. Campbell's hands flew to cover her mouth. "Please tell me Rita's okay. She was such a caring person. I don't know what she ever saw in that one." She pointed to Ricky who was still out cold on the front lawn.

An ambulance interrupted the conversation. It stopped in front of Mrs. Campbell's driveway. Two EMTs jumped out and surrounded Ricky. One police officer escorted the other EMT to the back of Rita's house.

Steve, the other officer, Delanie, and Mrs. Campbell moved out of the way next to the first police cruiser.

"Rita didn't make it, did she?" Mrs. Campbell asked quietly.

Delanie shook her head. "I'm so sorry about your friend. I was looking for the dog, and I found her in the shed behind the house."

"That sorry somebody. I hope he suffers as much as Rita did." She spat out the words in Ricky's general direction. "Y'all can take your time getting him to the hospital," she said over her shoulder. "And make sure you hit every pothole on your way over there."

"Mrs. Campbell, Officer Steele here is going to take your statement," Steve said. He opened the back door to his cruiser. "Delanie, you can sit here until I get back."

Delanie sat in the back seat with her feet on the asphalt. While Steve jogged around Rita's house, a forensic van, an animal control truck, and a dark-colored van joined the crowd of emergency vehicles. One of the officers cordoned off Rita's yard with yellow police tape. Neighbors gathered in small groups to watch, and Mrs. Campbell held court on her front porch.

After what seemed like hours, two guys loaded a gurney with a sheet over it into the dark-colored van as two local news crews turned onto the street. The police and forensic techs went in and out of Rita's house too many times to count. Finally, Steve and Officer Steele trotted over to the cruiser. Delanie stood as they approached.

"You doing okay?" Steve asked.

She nodded. "It's been a long day."

Steve showed Delanie a picture on his phone. "This Rita Meecham?"

Delanie nodded again. "Yes. What's next?"

"An officer went with the ambulance. He'll get Ricky Steeples's statement, and he'll be arrested for murder and a slew of other crimes when he's released from the emergency room. It may take a day or so. Mrs. Campbell did a number on his head. He's going to feel it for a while."

A slight smile crossed Officer Steele's face.

"I'm going to head out and return the dog. I'll send you my report," Delanie said.

"Okay. Keep me posted. We'll call you tomorrow if we have any other questions." Her brother held the door of the Mustang for her.

She pressed the button on her steering wheel. "Call Duncan."

"What's up? I thought you got lost," Duncan said.

"I was watching the forensic team at Rita's house. But before the police got there, I had a little run in with Ricky."

"You okay?"

"Yep. He banged on my car a little bit. No real damage. But the neighbor came out when he was yelling, and she clobbered him with a shovel."

Duncan snickered. "Neighborhood Watch at its finest."

"Yep. I'm headed your way. Are you at home or the office? We need to get Sid back to the West End."

"Meet me at the office. Sid and Margaret have been playing all afternoon, and Margaret's exhausted. Sid's a bundle of energy compared to her."

"See you in about fifteen minutes." Delanie put the windows down and cranked up a classic rock station. The drive and music would help clear her head.

CHAPTER SIX

Duncan and Delanie cruised down Rt. 288 to Elise Childress's house in Duncan's canary-colored Camaro. Both dogs napped in the tiny backseat.

"Thanks for keeping Sid safe," Delanie said. "I'm glad he wasn't with me when I encountered Ricky."

"Any word on old Ricky?"

Before she could answer, her phone buzzed. "Hey, Steve. What's up?" She clicked the button to put him on speaker phone.

"My forensic guys are still going through the house. They questioned Ricky at the hospital. It seems he's got some serious online gambling debts and needed cash. He told the detective that he hatched the idea for Rita to help him nab the dog to squeeze money out of her rich employer. He felt she could spare it, and it would be a quick way to get cash."

"So, she was in on it?" Delanie let out a sigh. She had hoped Rita was a victim in all this.

"At first. He said a day or so ago Rita wanted to return the dog. They got into a knock down drag out fight. Things turned ugly. Ricky insists that her death was an accident. He said he shoved her, and she fell and hit her head on the counter. We'll see what the medical examiner finds."

"But that got rid of the person who was supposed to do the money drop. He also botched the ransom notes. The one he mailed wasn't clear on when the handoff was going to take place."

"It must have been a better plan in his head. Nobody said

crooks were smart," Steve said. A police radio squawked in the background. "Where's the dog?"

"We're on our way to return him."

"Good. I'll call you tomorrow if there are any new developments."

"Thanks," she said as he disconnected.

Duncan frowned and signaled to exit at Broad Street. "Stupid crooks."

Delanie tilted her head. "They had no idea what they were doing. And they really didn't try to hide the dog. The neighbor told me she had seen it at the house."

"It makes our job easier."

"Turn at the next light and follow the road around for about a half-mile. Elise Childress's house is on the left. I filled her in on the phone. She's waiting anxiously for us. Well, for Sid anyway."

A few minutes later, Duncan pulled in the driveway. Before they could get Sid out of the back seat, Elise flung open the front door and ran down the stone steps. Sid jumped out of the car when he saw her and started barking. They did a happy dance that was punctuated with hugs and kisses.

"Thank you so much," she finally said to Delanie and Duncan. "I am eternally grateful to you both. And I will tell everyone I know how wonderful you are. You found my Sid and put that awful man in jail."

"I'm sorry about Rita."

Elise pursed her lips. "I trusted her, and she let me down. Rita, of all people. I can't believe she'd betray me like that. It's sad to say, but horrible things happen when you make bad choices. And now I have to find another housekeeper." She rolled her eyes and hugged Sid again. "Oh, here. I have your check." Elise pulled a slip of paper out of her blazer pocket. "Thanks again. Come on, Sid. We've got a lot of catching up to do. I am so sorry you had to spend time with those awful people. You're home now. Everything's going to be okay, baby."

The woman and her poodle climbed the steps and retreated into the house.

"He probably had the time of his life being a regular dog

with that yellow lab and Margaret. Another happy ending. Well, for Elise and Sid," Duncan said as he started the Camaro.

Delanie slid in the passenger seat and snapped her seatbelt in place. Not having any pressing work that demanded her time, she planned to head home and binge watch mindless television.

"Hey, I got some news for Sherlock Bones. I set up Margaret's online presence after her Pooch-a-palooza win. She's got quite a following now. I'm looking into some sponsorships and product reviews. She's already booked to appear at a doggie spa grand opening next month." Duncan signaled and pulled out of the neighborhood.

"Margaret the Wonder Dog. And I knew her before she became a celebrity. Is she going to want her own office?"

Duncan laughed, and Margaret opened one eye and snorted.

THE END

COMING SPRING 2022

The 4th Installment in the Mutt Mysteries Series

TO FETCH A KILLER

FOUR FUN "TAILS" OF CHAOS AND MURDER

More info at www.MuttMysteries.com

Be sure to LIKE Mutt Mysteries on Facebook

Follow @MuttMysteries1 on Twitter

TO FETCH A SCOUNDREL
Four Fun "Tails" of Scandal and Murder...

...is the second book in the Mutt Mysteries collection. It features four tail-wagging novellas. Each story puts pups' noses to the ground, as scandals are unleashed and killers are collared. Once you've finished reading these "tall-tails", you'll no longer wonder "Who let the dogs out?" You'll just be glad somebody did!

"The Fast and the Furriest"
by Heather Weidner

Cassidy Green just wants to keep her racetrack business from crashing. When an altercation breaks out between two race teams at the driver meeting, it adds one more problem to her already full plate. Cassidy gets more than she bargains for when Oliver, her Rottweiler, finds one of the star drivers dead in her garage. She hopes her fuzzy director of security will help uncover clues to reveal the killer before the bad publicity drives business into the wall.

"Pawsitively Scandalous"
by Jayne Ormerod

Pilar Pruitt and her black Lab Natti live in a community that has not had so much of a whisper of a crime in over sixty years. So, it's disconcerting when a neighbor is hauled off in handcuffs by the police for crimes unknown. But it's downright alarming when another dear friend is found dead. Pilar and Natti start digging deeper into residents' pasts, and the things they find are pawsitively scandalous!

"Ruff Goodbye"
by Rosemary Shomaker

Bar owner Len Hayes' frenemy Perry Lambert brings misery to all. Len finds himself strong-armed into shady business dealing by Winks family human attack dog Rocco Moretti, compliments of Perry. Len's grief over his best friend Curt's cancer death imbalances him, and everything unravels at Curt's funeral home visitation. The bar's stoic black Lab and Curt's miniature poodle have Len's back and resolve the mayhem.

"A Doggone Scandal"
by Teresa Inge

Catt Ramsey, owner of the Woof-Pack Dog Walkers, is back on the case when she receives a mysterious note in her pet supply order. Convinced the sender's motive is scandalous, Catt packs up her SUV and heads to the Outer Banks with her sister Em, family friend Jonathan Ray, and pups Cagney and Lacey to solve the mystery.

TO FETCH A THIEF
Four Fun "Tails" of Theft and Murder...

...is the first book in the Mutt Mysteries series and is comprised of four novellas that have gone to the dogs. In this howling good read, canine companions help their owners solve crimes and right wrongs. These sleuths may be furry and low to the ground, but their keen senses are on high alert when it comes to sniffing out clues and digging up the truth. Make no bones about it, these pup heroes will steal your heart as they conquer "ruff" villains.

"Hounding the Pavement"
by Teresa Inge

Catt Ramsey has three things on her mind: grow her dog walking service in Virginia Beach, solve the theft of a client's vintage necklace, and hire her sister Emma as a dog walker. But when Catt finds her model client dead after walking her precious dogs Bella and Beau, she and her own dogs Cagney and Lacey are hot on the trail to clear her name after being accused of murder.

"Diggin' up Dirt"
by Heather Weidner

Amy Reynolds and her Jack Russell Terrier Darby find some strange things in her new house. Normally, she would have trashed the forgotten junk, but Amy's imagination kicks into high gear when her nosy neighbors dish the dirt about the previous owners who disappeared, letting the house fall into foreclosure. Convinced that something nefarious happened, Amy and her canine sidekick uncover more abandoned clues in their search for the previous owners.

"It's a Dog Gone Shame!"
by Jayne Ormerod

Meg Gordon and her tawny terrier Cannoli are hot on the trail of a thief, a heartless one who steals rocks commemorating neighborhood dogs who have crossed the Rainbow Bridge. But sniffing out clues leads them to something even more merciless . . . a dead body! There's danger afoot as the two become entangled in the criminality infesting their small bayside community. It's a doggone shame, and Meg is determined to get to the bottom of things.

"This is Not a Dog Park"
by Rosemary Shomaker

"Coyotes and burglaries? That's an odd pairing of troubles." Such are Adam Moreland's reactions to a subdivision's meeting announcement. He has no idea. Trouble comes his way in spades, featuring a coyote . . . burglaries . . . and a dead body! A dog, death investigation, and new female acquaintance kick start Adam's listless life frozen by a failed relationship, an unfulfilling job, and a judgmental mother. Events shift Adam's perspective and push him to act.

Made in the USA
Middletown, DE
31 May 2023

31346281R00136